PENGUIN BOOKS

HUNGRY MEN

Edward Anderson was born in 1906, in Weatherford, Texas. His first novel, *Hungry Men*, published in 1935, was selected as the Doubleday/Doran Prize Novel. Anderson's next book, *Thieves Like Us*, served as the basis for the Altman film of the same name, and also inspired the film *They Live By Night*. Following a stint in Hollywood writing screenplays, Anderson settled in Brownsville, Texas, where he edited a local newspaper until his death in 1969.

HUNGRY MEN

Edward Anderson

PENGUIN BOOKS

PENGUIN BOOKS
Viking Penguin Inc., 40 West 23rd Street,
New York, New York 10010, U.S.A.
Penguin Books Ltd, Harmondsworth,
Middlesex; England
Penguin Books Australia Ltd, Ringwood,
Victoria, Australia
Penguin Books Canada Limited, 2801 John Street,
Markham, Ontario, Canada L3R 1B4
Penguin Books (N.Z.) Ltd, 182–190 Wairau Road,
Auckland 10, New Zealand

First published in the United States of America by
Doubleday, Doran & Co., Inc., 1935
Published in Penguin Books 1985

LIBRARY OF CONGRESS CATALOGING IN PUBLICATION DATA
Anderson, Edward, 1906–1969.
Hungry men.
I. Title.
PS3501.N218H8   1985   813'.52   84-26504
ISBN 0 14 00.7374 4

Printed in the United States of America by
R. R. Donnelley and Sons Company, Harrisonburg, Virginia
Set in Baskerville

Hungry Men was the first novel published by Edward Anderson, an American writer of the 1930s who is almost totally forgotten today, despite the curious persistence of his work in American culture. It was first published in 1935 by the firm of Doubleday, Doran as one of the two novels that year awarded a $1000 prize by *Story* magazine for the best novel-length work by a contributor to the magazine. (The other winner was Dorothy McCleary's *Not for Heaven*.) It was generally well received by the critics. Elizabeth Bowen said in the *New Statesman* that *Hungry Men* was "excellently written" and that "because of its matter of factness and gusto . . . it should certainly be read." Otis Ferguson in *The New Republic* said, "This is a well done, if episodic book, with a firm, quiet realism." The book was reprinted in pulp paperback editions in the fifties and early sixties, but it has remained out of print for more than a quarter of a century. It was only a piece by Geoffrey O'Brien in the "Save This Book" column of the *Village Voice Literary Supplement* that brought the book to the attention of Penguin editors.

What public recognition Anderson has enjoyed over the decades is due in large part to his second (and last) novel, *Thieves Like Us* (1937). A hard-boiled, laconic, yet suspenseful account of a small gang of bank robbers on the run in the American Southwest during the Depression, it received widespread acclaim—the *Saturday Review of Literature* going so far as to state that "it is not too much to say that Edward Anderson is the most exciting new figure to appear in American writing since Hemingway and Faulkner." *Thieves Like Us* served as the sole basis for two Hollywood feature films, Robert Altman's 1974 film of the same name and Nicholas Ray's *They Live By Night* (1948). It may also have served as at least partial inspiration for the several other Bonnie-and-Clyde–type films Hollywood has produced.

Nevertheless, Edward Anderson is today a writer whose works are in almost total eclipse. His name and the titles of his books are completely absent from the standard reference works of literary biography and the histories of thirties literature. We hope this paperback reissue will set in motion the process of rediscovery that will restore Anderson to a deserved place in American literary history.

Edward Anderson was born in 1906 in Weatherford, Texas, the son of a country printer. His family later moved to Oklahoma, where he went to school until his senior year of high school, when he left to take a cub reporter's job on a small daily paper in Ardmore, Oklahoma. There followed a peripatetic decade of wandering throughout Texas, Arkansas, and Oklahoma, for the most part working on newspapers, but also with brief stints as a deckhand on a freighter, a prizefighter, and a trombone player. Simultaneously Anderson began writing fiction, but the only sales he made were of boxing and detective stories to pulp magazines.

In 1931, disgusted with his inability to sell his stories, Anderson began riding the rails. Starting from a Memphis railroad yard, his odyssey took him from Chicago to New York to Florida to New Orleans—and face to face with the human devastation of the Depression. Here is how he described his experience for *Story*:

> I rode the "blinds" of crack passenger trains, freight manifests and slow locals: in gondolas and cattle cars: slept in welfare flops, 10-cent hotels, parks and darkened churches. Day after day, month after month, season after season. I met bums in Battery Park of New York that I had jungled up with in Mountain Air, Arkansas. Not all the time did I feel like a gen'l'man with guts. Sometimes I felt like a dog with distemper.

The experience set Anderson to thinking about the politics of the situation:

Every idle man becomes economic-minded. He starts wanting to know why this man has a chauffeured Packard and he can't get his three-dollar shoes half-soled? But the American isn't going to turn Socialist or Communist. At least not in this generation. I wanted to write something to explain it.

In 1934, Anderson left the road for good, got married, and moved to New Orleans, where he began writing again. He was able to sell true detective stories to the pulps while *Story* published a hobo piece of his, "Guy in the Blue Overcoat," which brought in a great volume of mail. His career as a writer was finally launched.

Unfortunately, Anderson's spell as a novelist was brief: He never published another novel after *Thieves Like Us*. In 1937, the year of its publication, Anderson moved to Hollywood, where he worked as a contract screenwriter, first for Paramount Studios and then for Warner Brothers. It was not a happy experience for Anderson, so he went back to reporting, first in California for the *Los Angeles Examiner* and the *Sacramento Bee*, and after 1946 for a succession of papers in his native Texas. In the last two decades of his life Anderson became increasingly alienated and removed, evolving a radical personal philosophy compounded of populism, anti-Communism, and the Swedenborgian religion. In his final years he settled in Brownsville, Texas, where he edited the Harlingen, Texas, paper and wrote a local newspaper column. He continued to write fiction, but never attempted to place his manuscripts. He died in 1969, at the age of sixty-three, in almost total obscurity.

CONTENTS

CONTENTS

HUNGRY MEN

1

The Starvation Army

The weak bubble of the mission's water fountain and its flat, swimming-hole taste washed away the dull satisfaction that had been Acel Stecker's on reaching the free shelter. He straightened slowly, wiping his mouth on the shoulder of his corduroy jacket, and looked around him with a smoldering hostility.

The afternoon shade was lengthening into the baking side street. Bums sat on the curb, their backbones arched like drawn bows; squatted against the mission's scaly walls, dragged aimlessly around in that calloused weariness that men of the road know. Some of them had that faded cleanliness that the dark washrooms of flop houses give, but there were others, like Acel Stecker, with lusterless, bloodveined eyes to which the cinders and dirt of freight-train travel still clung.

The eyes of the man approaching the fountain were watery, as if overflowing with the soup he had consumed, and his face was dry and brown like a crust of begged bread. Acel moved aside for him and, watching, saw the shoulder blades push up the sweat-streaked denim shirt in two sharp ridges. Flabby lips hid the bubble and made animal noises in drinking. Acel turned away. . . .

The damned lice, he thought. There's no getting away from them. They're the same everywhere. In Denver and El Paso, Pittsburgh, Los Angeles, Atlanta . . .

A man with a raw, shaven face came up and squinted at Acel uncertainly. "Ain't you the guy I saw on the *Bullet* outa Portland about two weeks ago?" he said.

Acel nodded. "I came out of Portland. I remember you now. You're the A. B. I was talking to."

The seaman brought out a Prince Albert tobacco can and shook two cigarette butts out of it into the palm of his hand. "You didn't stay over in Baltimore, uh?" He extended his palm, and Acel took the shorter of the butts.

"I didn't have a chance gettin' out of Baltimore. Those tankers were just taking on company men, and their discharges couldn't be more than six months old."

"Well, you've hit a no-good bastard now," the seaman said.

"Washington?"

"The bonusers put this town on the bum."

"I heard this was a good town."

They went over and sat down on the curb. The seaman had a naked woman tattooed on his forearm. He began to clench and unclench his hand, and they watched, abstractedly, the suggestive wriggling of the tattoo's belly.

"So this town's no good?" Acel said.

The seaman let his arm drop. He said that yesterday he had lost his buddy. The buddy had put the bing on a plainclothesman on the capitol grounds and was in jail now for panhandling.

"I just hoofed it out to the end of Pennsylvania Avenue and put the bum on a priest out there," Acel said.

"Didn't you have any luck?"

"Not the sweat under his arms."

They watched the peanut vendor work his cart against the curb across the street. The vendor took three bags and arranged them on the cart's top.

The seaman said he had been staying in the mission for a week. He was trying to get a pair of shoes. "You got to do a nose dive," he said. "You know what I mean. Go up in front while they're singing and kneel down and let 'em pray over you. I haven't done it yet, but I think I'll do it tonight. There's a Jew here that's got shoes and breeches, and he come here the same day I did."

A line began forming at the entrance, and the seaman told Acel they were registering the new transients and he'd better get up there.

The man at the registration desk had a bleached, womanish face. He wrote with a stub of a pencil and screwed up his mouth when he crossed letters.

There were eight men ahead of Acel in the line leading to the desk. I don't mind this registering business so much, he thought. I gripe out on the road about having to go through all this red tape for a bowl of soup, but I don't mind this so much. I guess it's because I like to have somebody ask me questions. It's an illusion that somebody is interested in me personally. Who is interested in me? The government. That's because I am a social menace. That's being something, anyway. But that old belch there doesn't care who I am or where I slept last night. Maybe that's why I lie like I do. I'll tell this old boy I'm a prize fighter. I was a dish washer in Columbus.

"What is your name?" the registrar said.

"Acel Stecker."

"How old are you?"

"Twenty-five."

"Religion?"

"I don't have any."

The registrar looked up, and his lips tightened. "You have to have one to stay here."

"Make it Protestant, then."

Dusk veiled the mission street. It shadowed the road-seared faces and blurred their shabbiness. Men moved closer together and talked more boldly and laughed. Down on the corner the portable organ was groaning in a street service preliminary to the services that were to be held in a few minutes in the mission.

Acel was directed to a bench on the left of the altar, a place designated for the transients spending their first night in the shelter. He sat there and held the soiled hymn book in both hands.

The preacher was a tall man with long jaws on a bony neck. The hollows under his jaws could pocket golf balls. He smiled now and patted the hymn book in his hand. "It is good to sing, brothers. Let's turn now to that old favorite, 'He Lifted Me.' "

A boy in a torn white shirt sat next to Acel. He nudged Acel now and exhibited the hymn title to which he had scrawled: *Into a Mission.* Acel winked in mock gravity and looked back up at the preacher.

On the platform in a wide half-circle of yellow, cane-bottomed chairs sat a dozen men. They were men of middle ages and with coats and trousers that matched, and some of them had watch chains across their vests. After the first song the collection plate was passed, and these men were the only ones who dropped coins.

The boy next to Acel sang in a falsetto tenor and then in a croaking bass. He would look up to Acel from time to time for approval. The man on Acel's left held the last note of each verse as if he wanted to convince everyone he was singing.

After the singing the preacher read from the Bible: "And he would fain have filled his belly with the husks that the swine did eat; and no man gave unto him."

I ought to listen to this sermon on the prodigal son, Acel thought. Time would pass by quicker. But I've heard this sermon a hundred times.

"I know, brothers," the preacher said, "that some of you out there may think that you do not have much to be thankful for, because you do not have jobs or money—at least I don't have any money; but what I want to tell you is that you do have something to be thankful for. You do have something to be thankful for. You have the chance to accept Him."

The man with the yellow shoes and white cotton socks seated at this end of the half-circle said, "Amen."

"No man in this world can ask for more than the opportunity of accepting Him," the preacher said. "He will provide, brothers, and all you have to do is place yourself in His hands and He will take care of you."

I wonder what kind of husks the prodigal son wanted to eat, Acel thought. Were they the kind of husks that tamales are wrapped in? I don't see how a man could eat them. . . .

With the sermon's conclusion the preacher invited members of the gathering desiring special prayer to come forward while the gathering sang, and kneel down before the altar. "I want you to come down and feel Him in your heart," he said. "Don't be ashamed in the presence of God. You must stand before Him some day, and then you must be able to say, 'I accepted You on earth, Lord.' Come forward, brothers, while we sing, and get down on your knees before Him."

Men got up and lurched noisily forward. They bumped into one another in their haste to take kneeling places before the altar. Acel looked for the seaman, but he was not among the nose divers.

After the special prayer the kneeling men were told to rise, and then they were directed to sit on a bench at the messroom entrance.

The preacher was less solemn now. He moved lightly about on the platform and smiled again. "We have some visitors with us tonight," he said, "some men who have honored our little house of worship with their presence."

The men in the cane-bottomed chairs sat more erect. Yellow Shoes blew his nose.

"These men, I am proud to say," the preacher said, "are

Christly men, men who walk in His footsteps. I am going to call upon them to say a few words to you, and let me tell you out there, brothers, that you are in for a treat, because these men here can tell you out of their own experiences just what He means to you."

Yellow Shoes came forward. He had the poise of a man who had talked to many gatherings like this and pretty soon was gesturing like the preacher.

"Brothers, I want to tell you that I'm a man forty-eight years of age and a happy man, and what I want to tell you is that for forty years of my life I lived in the darkness," Yellow Shoes said. "Now you wouldn't do that, would you? Live forty years in the darkness like a blind man? But that's what I did, and all the time, brothers, I could have lived in the light. I don't mind confessing to you out there that I was a drinker of whisky once. I caroused around, and I thought I was having a good time, and all the time I was living in the darkness. I didn't know what it meant to be happy, but, brothers, I finally saw the light. It was eight years ago the fourteenth of last month and, brothers, I want you to know that He can show you the light, too."

"Ah-men," the preacher said.

"Glory to God," the man in the chair next to that vacated by Yellow Shoes shouted.

"And I don't want you to miss forty years of your life like I did," Yellow Shoes said. "Don't live in the darkness. Don't deny yourself the great good He can give."

"Ah-men."

"Glory to God!"

Acel stared at the floor, his arms folded across his chest. The kid was sharpening his knife on his shoe again. It's after ten o'clock now, Acel thought. Now there goes another up there to spout off glory-to-god stuff. The bastards. Do they think anybody here wants to hear that stuff? Can't they find anybody else to tell it to, besides a bunch of bums who came in here to get something to eat and a place to flop? A little singing is all right, and a little preaching don't hurt, but this is carrying it into the ground. Now there's another one gettin' up. The bastard. There ought to be a law against this. Gentlemen of the jury, is this right? Look at this, gentlemen of the jury. This is the case of Hungry Men against Men Who Live in the Light. See yonder gentlemen, the closed front door. That means no bum is going to enter this place now because he hasn't paid the price of listening to these holy men. Observe the holy nose divers there. Why did they trot up there and get down on their knees? Don't bull me. It wasn't for salvation, but to be first in the soup line and maybe get a pair of shoes. What do you call this? Isn't this forcing religion down throats that want soup? Religion is for full bellies and for men who can drop coins in a plate. . . .

It ended at last, like night rides in the Rockies; like tunnels and searing cinders; as all hardships of the road end.

They were handed bowls of navy-bean soup and three slices of bread. They ate standing at long, plank tables, swiftly and ravenously, and lifted tin bowls to their mouths to get the last half-spoonful. Then they bolted, like fugitives, into the street.

The youth in the white shirt and black bow tie announced to the cluster of first nighters in front of the mission: "We're taking you first nighters to another place tonight. Aw right, you guys, follow me, single file."

He set off in a fast walk, and some of the men had to trot to catch up. He led them across the courthouse park, down the street and past another park. Idlers in front of drugstores stared.

Anybody could have come up, Acel thought, and told this bunch to fall in line and we'd have fell in. Anybody in a clean shirt and slicked hair. All he would have had to say was, "Fall in" and we would follow him the rest of the night, to Alexandria even.

It was a big, empty building with a clean, fresh-paint

smell. In its cool bareness the voices of the first nighters sounded deep and free. The washroom was on the fourth floor, and the men, after undressing on the second floor, walked naked up the tickling cement stairway. After the shower they returned to the dormitory of cots.

Acel lay on his cot and ran his hand slowly through his damp hair. The bare feet of men returning from the showers padded on the cement floor.

"Somebody strike a match so I can find the light in this place," a voice said, and there was laughter.

Men sat on the edges of their cots, picked their toes and talked to men around them. Acel listened to the voices:

"Bulls are sure gettin' tough in Pittsburgh. I saw one gun-whip the hell out of a guy. They weren't so tough about a year ago when I was through there. I was there when those four boys in that gondola were killed."

"I got a real sit-down this morning in Richmond. Ham and eggs and pie. The old woman told me she had a boy on the road."

"The guy who says you can't blind the Twentieth Century is crazy as hell 'cause I sure held it down. . . . Water on the fly . . . last winter . . . four of 'em . . . chopped 'em out with an axe . . ."

"Texas Slim ain't so tough . . . Denver Bob . . . One-armed Kelly . . . The Gila Monster . . . Did you hear about . . . ? They was waitin' for him in the car, and when he stuck his head in the door they slammed it on him. Drove spikes in his hands and through his feet and one up his backside."

Acel had impulses to sit up and join in the road gossip. He could tell them about that Negro bull some bums had dropped a coupling on. The Kid, lying on the next cot, turned over again restlessly, and Acel opened his eyes and half sat up: "Well, good-night, Kid."

The Kid raised up on his stomach and looked at Acel. "I just couldn't keep from thinking about it all the time he was preaching. Why in the hell didn't that prodigal son kill them hogs and eat?"

2

THE WINDOW BUSTER

THE morning shade of the park trees covered Acel like a cool sheet. Curled on the thin grass, he watched, with screwed-up eyes, the tiny ant struggling through the hairy forest of his forearm. Whitey, the Californian, had left him to rummage for newspapers in the park waste cans. It was a relief for Whitey to be gone awhile. The Californian had two rigid creases between his eyes, as if he were continually trying to work out a mathematical problem.

I wonder what the name of this park is, Acel thought. I've been in a lot of parks I don't know the name of. I've been in Central Park and Boston Common and Grant Park and the Plaza in El Paso and Lafayette Square and Pershing Square. I've been in a lot of parks. Is that what I can boast about now? That I've been in a lot of parks? Is that a bum's treasure?

How long have I been running around the country now? Two years. Damn near two years. It has been two years since I played in that Juarez cabaret. Godamighty. Two years I been on the bum. I thought I was too good for that Spick's orchestra in Juarez, and that's why he fired me. I was a lot better than the rest of them. I'd played in a lot better bands. It would have scared me to death then if somebody had said: "You won't even have a job two years from now." I didn't have any guts then, though. . . .

Whitey, the Californian, dropped the newspapers on the

grass and then, his bony knees popping, bumped into a cross-legged sitting position. His scalp was pink and slick-looking underneath his straw-colored hair. He began flipping the sheets of the spread newspaper, as if he expected something concealed in the folds to jump out at him.

"I just decided to go back to New York," Acel said.

"Whatchu going to do up there?"

"I'm going to get a job. There's a fellow up there from my home town who's a pretty big shot in the music game. I'm going to look him up and tell him I need a job."

"When you thinking about going?"

"In the morning. I'm thinking about highwaying it."

"That town's too big for me. There's nothing up there for me."

They watched the man in the pearl flannel suit and ribboned panama hat go by on the walk.

"You know when I was a kid," Acel said, "I used to think hunger was something like the toothache, only worse. I mean when you went a long time. But now I know there isn't much to it."

"All hunger is, is your belly muscles drawing up."

"Yeah, a man could starve to death and not know it."

"You'd flop over before you starved to death. I saw one do it yesterday around at the Sally. I thought he was drunk for a minute, the way he was staggerin' around. He hit the floor like a ton of bricks, but he was all right after they fed him. Goddamit, though, that's not right. I'm going to bust me a window yet. Work you six hours a day in the woodyard and feed you twice, and what they feed you there isn't any nutrition in it. I'm always hungry as hell an hour after breakfast."

"The thing that bothers you, Whitey, is you havin' to stick here for that mail. I know how it is. I sure get ants when I have to stay in a spot long."

"That bud of mine is a horse's behind. Been on that fire department for ten years and never been out of Southern

California. He don't know what it is to be out of a job. He
may not even answer my letter."

The boy in white duck trousers with the ice-cream box
slung across his shoulder looked at them but did not pause.

"That's what makes you so sore, waitin' on that mail,"
Acel said. "When a man is on the move it isn't so bad. I
know that that's a fact. A man on the road has something
to look forward to even if it's just the next town. And you're
so busy going that you don't have time to think about how
tough things are. No man thinks about dying much, and
that's because he's too busy worrying about keeping alive."

"What I'd like to do," Whitey said, "is find that son of a
bitch that stole my drawers last night. I watched everybody
dress this morning, but I didn't see 'em. I'm gonna watch
again tonight."

"A man that would steal a bum's drawers would spit on
a church altar," Acel said. "That makes me think about
that suit of mine I got in New York in the Seafarers'. I got
to raise a couple of bucks some place to get them cleaned
up. I got to get a shirt, too, somehow. If I'm going to look
up Red Gholson I got to have a front. I can't look like a
bum."

A rain-heralding draft swept across the park and stirred
the spread newspaper. Whitey slapped the sheets back down
and tapped the big photograph on the society page with a
firm forefinger. "Look at this bunch of women," he said.

Acel got up and looked over his shoulder. The débu-
tantes looked like movie actresses with their curving hips
and firm breasts and poised smiles.

Whitey tapped the photograph again. "They may be
dressed up and lookin' fine, but their armpits stink the
same as mine."

Acel got up, loosened his belt, and began stuffing in his
shirt tail.

"Where you going?" Whitey said.

"C'mon, let's go bum us something to eat. I'm not hittin'

that penny joint this time, though. They worked me two hours in that joint yesterday, and they didn't give me a dime's worth to eat. I'm going to hit a hotel."

"It's only about two hours now until the Sally feeds."

"I got to eat good today. I'm going to do a bunch of walking gettin' out of this town in the morning, and I want to feel pretty good."

3

UP FROM THE STOCKYARDS

ACEL trudged in that heel-dragging walk of the hitch hiker who has miles to go and is in no particular hurry to get there. The hot morning sun tingled in the roots of his bare head, and he held his eyes down, watching the toes of his scarred shoes.

He asked the man standing at the corner bus station: "Am I going right, mister, to hit the Baltimore highway?"

The stranger gave the directions in detail—the boulevard, the stop lights, the school—but Acel only half listened to the latter part. It was easier to ask someone else later on than remember all the directions. Sometimes he would walk miles out of his way for not remembering, but it was a nuisance watching for direction marks.

He moved on, down the sidewalks of a long, wide street. There were young trees in the parkways and smooth, green lawns. There were white frame houses with green shutters and compact brick houses with bright deck chairs on the porches. The houses and the lawns moved past him as if he were standing still, so insensible was he to physical effort.

Just ahead of him a youth in a blue turtle-neck sweater ran across the walk and bounded onto the running board of a new roadster. He was tanned like saddle leather. A girl sat behind the wheel of the mirrory car smoking a cigarette.

A good bum, Acel thought, would approach the fellow and put the bing on him. A fellow with a girl makes a good touch. He could go up and say: "Bud, could you help a man who hasn't had anything to eat today?"

The roadster shot off with a quick shifting of gears.

How long have I been walking now? Acel thought. Two . . . three hours? It is the wear on shoes and the fuel it takes that matters in hiking. It's going to be noon before I even get to the highway. If there should be a revolution, on whose side would the fellow in the hot sweater be? Would the revolution be between fellows in cotton pants like myself and fellows in sweaters with girls in shiny roadsters? Would the revolutionists say that all men who lived in houses that cost more than ten thousand dollars were their enemies? But men in ten-thousand-dollar houses needn't worry about bums revolting. They don't have guts. Look at me. If somebody came along and picked me up, I'd think the world was level. If I was a revolutionary leader, though, I'd like to have one of these rich bastards come before me. I'd say: "Did you ever give a bum a lift? No. Take him out. Off with his head!"

Hunger seized him almost without warning and with a vicious, shaking grip. It was as if a draining needle had been plunged into him and now his strength-emptied body trembled in outraged protest. He was a little awed. "Now this is hunger, real, sure-enough hunger," he said half aloud.

Across the street was a beauty shop with an orchid front. A woman with her hair plastered down and in a net came out and got into a sedan. At the fountain of the drugstore a man on a stool sipped through a straw. The screen doors of the grocery store slammed as a man smoking a cigar came out.

Acel lifted his hand and watched it tremble. There was oatmeal left in that bowl in the Sally this morning and he should have eaten it all. He had told himself so at the time.

This was hunger, all right. It wasn't illness, because he was thinking about oatmeal. That truck driver who picked him up last summer: "When I pick one up and they begin to talk about how long it is since they've eaten, I say to 'em, 'I got a nickel here, Mac, and I'll get us a loaf of bread and we'll split it.' And then I gets the bread, and if they eat that, then I know they're hungry, and at the next diner I buy 'em a real feed."

I'm trembling like I did when I come down out of the capitol dome yesterday. There's no use of me standing here like this. I'll go in that grocery yonder.

Acel entered the store, and when he reached its center he stopped and looked around at the clerks. A little man in billowy sleeves approached in a little lope.

"Do you have some old bread, mister?"

The little man turned quickly, but his movements after that were unhurried, and he went to the screen door at the back and spoke to someone above. "Bread," Acel heard him say.

Acel watched the little man. I'm going to rate something all right, because I heard him say, "Bread." I heard him say that.

The man brought out a roll of lunch meat from the icebox and cut three slices. He left the icebox and went up front, but Acel kept looking at the icebox.

The little man handed Acel the paper sack. "Thank you," Acel said. The man did not say anything, and Acel twisted his head. "Many thanks to you, sir."

He was outside of the store now with the paper sack in his hand. He walked toward the highway, and it was as if something were prodding him in the back and if he walked fast he might escape its pressure.

There was a tree on the left of the highway, and it curved out at the trunk. It was shady, and the curve fitted his back. Everything is working fine now. Right here on the highway and a good tree and a sack of something to eat. One . . .

two . . . three sandwiches. Tomatoes! By god, the old boy put in some bananas!

After he had eaten, Acel got up and stood at the edge of the highway. He felt strength in the breadth of his chest and the slope of his shoulders, in the steadiness of his legs and the firmness of his stomach. He stood there on the highway that curled northward like a long grey ribbon and thumbed with rhythmic boldness.

The big moving truck approached slowly, but when Acel thumbed, the driver shook his head and spread his hands apologetically. Acel nodded and saluted understandingly. He watched the truck lumber on up the highway. I know, bud, it isn't you. It's the insurance companies, and you'd lose your job if they caught you picking somebody up.

The tires of the long sedan sung on the pavement. A girl in the rear looked back through the glass and smiled. Acel waved. He double-shuffled and hooked a left and crossed a right.

Machines came in rushes: a Lincoln with a Negro chauffeur and two toady women in floppy straw hats. A driver with a cigar, clinging stiffly to the wheel. A farmer in a Model T, and two machines with running boards loaded and California licenses.

There were lulls with the highway emptied and silent, and Acel stirred the gravel with his toe or tossed pebbles at the telephone pole on the other side.

A hitch hiker with a canvas bag came up and set his bag down. He had on a tan flannel suit with patch pockets. "How long you been holding this spot down?" he said.

"About an hour, I guess," Acel said. "You have a smoke on you?"

The other produced a cellophane pack.

"Tailor-mades," Acel said. "Been a long time since I smoked a good cigarette."

"I was six hours on a spot yesterday," the newcomer said. "I was thumbing everything that passed me, too, women and everything. I hope I get out of this place pretty soon."

Acel exhaled with a quick upward jerk of his head. "I ride trains mostly when I'm traveling, but I'm only trying to make Baltimore today, and I thought I'd highway it. I don't like this thumbing myself."

"I may get a bus when I get to Baltimore. I've been three days now from Richmond, and at this rate I'm not going to save very much gettin' to Boston. I may just get a bus."

"If you got a few bucks you might as well hang onto them. A ride might come along here and take you clear into Boston. I wouldn't spend any bus money."

There was a rush of cars, and Acel thumbed half-heartedly.

"The trouble with them," the hitch hiker said, "is that they're afraid of getting hijacked. That's just their excuse. They just don't want to stop and fool with you."

"That's it."

"If it wasn't that I wouldn't have a cent when I got to Boston I would get a bus and say to hell with them, but I just have a few dollars, and I need them when I get there."

"If a man will just be patient a ride will come along. I get sore as hell sometimes and wish one of them would turn over down the road after he passed and then yell for somebody to come and pull the car off of him. I guess he'd let you do that, all right."

"Women never do pick you up. You ever had a woman pick you up?"

"Once or twice. I never do thumb women. They're afraid they'll get raped, I guess."

The hitch hiker picked up his bag. "I guess I'll go on down the road. Two of us together won't do any good. This hiking is like sticking your tail out and every time somebody passes they kick it."

In just a few minutes the black sedan stopped, and for several moments Acel did not think the driver was stopping for him. He had been made foolish a lot of times by drivers who were simply going to turn around. But this driver was opening the door!

The driver had on pinch-nose glasses, and his middle-aged face had a barber-shop freshness. When they settled in high gear he said:

"Where you going, young man?"

"I'm going to New York."

"You are not a New Yorker, are you?"

"No, sir." Acel reached out and waved at the hitch hiker in the flannel suit. "No, sir, but I'm going to be if I get this job I'm planning on."

"You are from the South, aren't you?"

"Well, Oklahoma. I was born in Oklahoma."

Acel shook his head when the other offered cigarettes. They rode in silence. Acel extended his feet a little and slid down on the cushions.

The driver made a sweeping gesture with his hand. "Yonder across that water there is going to be a bridge soon, and it will be a vision fulfilled. That span will connect two communities, and it will be a dream realized. It is to be a reality, too, because the government has appropriated the money, just about, and construction will start soon. One man dreamed that bridge and planned it for a long time, and soon he will see his vision take form."

Acel looked at the driver a little furtively. The other spoke as if he were addressing an audience and with a careful selection of words. Acel cleared his throat. "Who is the man?"

"I am the man." The driver rapped on the steering wheel with the palm of his hand. "I am the man."

"You are going to build a bridge over there?"

"I visioned that bridge five years ago."

"Oh, I see. You're an engineer."

"No, I am chairman of the Chamber of Commerce bridge committee."

"Oh, I see."

"You can do the same, young man. Don't think there is not opportunity in this world. I started out working when

I was twelve years old in the old Kansas City stockyards. I worked in the stockyards for a mere pittance when I was a boy and on top of that was practically an invalid. I had an operation, and for two years I had a hose running out of my belly. And I worked right in those stockyards with that hose in my belly until the boss saw that I wasn't physically able to do that kind of work and put me in the office. I couldn't add two and two, but I tackled it and began studying nights. . . ."

Acel slid farther down in the seat and folded his arms. A mushed cat lay on the pavement ahead, and he flinched as he felt the car's wheels bump on the carcass.

"I worked very hard in that office. I didn't know what hours were. They made me a clerk, and I worked at that about a year and then had to have a new operation. I had my eye on a salesman's job all the time, though, and when I got that, the first month I made more sales than any other young man on the force."

Acel recrossed his legs. I ought to pay more attention to what this man is saying, because he might ask me a question in a minute. He must be somebody, all right.

". . . sent to Fort Worth . . . man for the job . . . big interests . . . merger . . . opportunity . . . St. Louis . . . sweet little girl . . . married . . . Oklahoma City . . . apartment . . . five hundred dollars saved . . . hard row . . . while I was gone the man that lived in the apartment across the hall tried to make my wife . . . business picked up . . ."

I'll say to Gholson: "I'm Acel Stecker, Mr. Gholson, from Bovina City. I just got in New York and I'd like to see you." He'll let me come up, I'll bet, telling him I'm from Bovina City. I should have looked him up before. I don't see why I didn't think of that before. . . .

". . . Kansas City . . . office in shape . . . fifty-per-cent increase . . . Philadelphia . . . merger . . . vice-president . . . Packers' Association . . . you can do the same, young man."

". . . It was like this, Mr. Gholson, I didn't know times

were going to be so hard, so I quit the Apaches and with a few hundred I'd saved worked my way to Europe. I knew your dad pretty well, Mr. Gholson. If you will give me a tip on a job, I sure will appreciate it. If you will suggest somewhere I could try, I'd appreciate it a whole lot. If I could just get a couple of nights a week, I'd certainly appreciate it."

A coupé approached, and the driver suddenly stiffened and leaned out of his car and waved wildly. "That was old Jock Early," he said to Acel. "Insurance man. Fine a fellow as ever lived."

Acel nodded.

"I have a boy about your age in Columbia. Have a girl, too. She's in California now. I say let them do what they want to . . . Insurance . . . Rotarian . . . Chamber of Commerce . . . Well, I'll let you out here, young man."

Acel stirred up with the alertness of a man who has been caught napping. They were at the outskirts of the city.

"I turn this way here," the driver said. He reached across and twisted the door out. "Sorry I can't take you any farther."

Acel slid out. "Many thanks, mister, for the lift."

"That's perfectly all right, son. Remember, now, you can do the same."

4
"Boats"

WITH the roll of tabloid newspapers under his arm, Acel stood there on the walk looking across darkened Battery Park at the still forms which lay scattered on the grass like corpses on a battlefield. A train crashed around the elevated curve toward South Ferry. Ship horns groaned on the East River, on the Hudson, and in the Bay. The traffic of lower Broadway ground on like a giant unoiled machine.

He stepped over the strand of wire separating the walk from the grass and moved across the black carpet. He chose a spot distant from the other sleepers and spread the newspapers. After removing his shoes and tying the laces, he covered them with his jacket for a pillow. He lay on his back and looked up at the swirling heavens. . . .

The girl's laugh, excited and repressed, made him stir up on his elbow and look about. Just a few yards away a couple were spreading newspapers. The youth was bareheaded, and the sleeves of his white shirt were rolled high on his biceps. The girl, lifting her dress a little, went to her knees and then fell around to sit beside him. Acel turned on his side in order to watch them.

The couple lay on the papers now, but presently the girl sat up, her chin on her knees. The youth chuckled and then, grasping her, pulled her down to him. Their mouths met, the girl with teasing pecks. Suddenly the youth grasped her fiercely, and then they clung in possessive embrace. . . .

The draft blowing over the Bay and across Battery Park was moist and chilling. Acel awoke with the back of his hand lying in the wet grass. He placed it between his legs and hunched tighter, but it was no use. He sat up, shivering, and fumbled with shaking fingers for cigarette papers. When he had the cigarette burning he put on his shoes and jacket and moved toward South Ferry.

Bums slept on all the benches, some of them wrapped in newspapers. He peered into the bandstand, but its floor was covered with human bundles.

On the illuminated walk near the ferry buildings there was a bench of men. They were talking and laughing. Acel sat down on an adjoining bench, and presently a short, stocky youth in wide-bottomed, blue denim trousers came over. "Spare another smoke, mate?"

Acel handed him the sack.

The youth had gold teeth. "Been sleeping in the park?"

Acel nodded. "It's too cold, I couldn't sleep."

The other handed him the sack. "If you get on a bench and wrap up with papers it isn't so bad."

"Try and find a bench, though."

"I'm going to turn in pretty soon, and if you want to I'll show you where you can flop. It's warm, anyway."

Gold Teeth returned to the other bench. "They can kidnap them all if they want to," he said. "What are those rich guys to me? They wouldn't spit on me if my guts were on fire."

Acel went over and stood at the end of the bench of men.

"None of these rich bastards ever did anything for me," Gold Teeth said. "They can kidnap every damned one of 'em."

The man at the end of the bench made room for Acel. He had on clean, khaki work clothing. His clean-shaven face had a rich, healthy coloring. "I haven't seen you around here before," he said.

"No, I just got off the road this afternoon. I been in this town before, though."

"Well, a man won't starve here." He got up and picked up a cigarette butt off the walk. He was short and built like a fire plug.

Acel brought out his tobacco sack. "I got tobacco here, buddy."

"Save your tobacco." The man pulled out a pipe and crammed the broken butt into it.

Gold Teeth kept talking. He said he had quit looking for work. The field was too overcrowded. He looked at the man beside Acel. "Ain't I right, Boats?"

"Stay in there," Boats said. Aside he said to Acel: "That fellow is a character. Gorki or London could have used him. Tully, too."

Acel nodded.

"That is the type that will furnish the drive and power for the revolution. They don't think, but they have the guts."

"Why, do you think there is going to be a revolution?"

"Of a certainty. Just as soon as the men on this bench and the men on benches all over the country realize why they're jobless. Then the revolution will come. But the masses haven't been aroused yet. They feel that something is wrong, but they are too stupid to understand why."

"I don't see much chance for a revolution myself," Acel said.

Boats looked at Acel. "Why don't you think there is much chance?"

"Oh, I don't know. I haven't thought about it so much, to tell the truth."

"That's it, then, comrade. The average man doesn't think about it. The average man is just an alimentary canal with a billiard ball for a head."

"You know what it's all about, then, uh?" Acel spat scornfully between his teeth.

"At least I think about it, comrade. I don't sit around and pick my nose and say, 'This country is all right. I'll get mine some day.' "

"Well, friend, I'm not shouting hurrah for the kidnapers, and neither do I intend to be like this the rest of my life."

Gold Teeth beckoned. "C'mon, you two, let's go."

Boats waved him back. "We'll go in a minute." He looked at Acel again. "No, you won't be a bum all the time. All this is temporary to you, I suppose. I guess you're having a pretty good time."

"Nope, this isn't my idea of a good time."

"I can't see how a man can live this sort of life and fail to see the injustice of the governmental system that spawns it. Now you——"

"Forget it, bud. You don't know anything about me."

"I'm going, you guys," Gold Teeth said. "If you're going now, let's go."

Boats and Acel followed Gold Teeth. They crossed lower Broadway. Out of the cigar store at the corner came a youth in white linen trousers and a yellow silk polo shirt. Gold Teeth stopped him. "How about a cigarette, Queenie?"

Queenie tossed his head. "Sorry, I'm trying to make a dollar myself tonight."

They walked on, and Boats winked at Acel. "You're too ugly, Goldie."

Gold Teeth laughed. "Yeah, I'm just too ugly."

Sleeping forms lay in building entrances and on the slanting doors of coal chutes. "American seamen," Boats said and gestured with mock dramatism. "Galley slaves were at least taken care of when they weren't at sea, but a capitalistic slave when he isn't working sleeps in the street. And they talk about Russia."

"Well, what are you going to do about it?" Acel said.

"Little matches make big fires, comrade."

"What these guys ought to do is get 'em some six-shooters and get it," Gold Teeth said.

They turned into a darkened alley and moved up it single file. Halfway up the block, Gold Teeth stopped and then, agile as a monkey, climbed up and disappeared through a narrow opening in the boarded window of the big building.

"This is the Hoover Hotel," Boats said, and he followed Gold Teeth.

Acel pulled himself up to the ledge and then squeezed through the aperture. It was dark as a ship's hold inside, and for several moments he stood there like a man blindfolded. The feet of his companions scraped ahead. He lowered himself to the gritty cement floor and then moved across it in the direction of their sounds. The place smelled of charred wood and human bodies.

Acel could see a little better now. He stood at the foot of a fire-razed, skeleton stairway. He no longer heard his companions. He started up the stairway, and once he touched a charred beam that had fallen across it, and its crust loosened.

He peered into rooms on the second floor. Light from a street lamp filtered through the boarded window cracks on the forms of sleeping men. There were no spots here.

Acel climbed on up to the next floor, but here too the newspaper-covered floors were strewn with sleeping hulks. On the fifth floor he found a spot and, carefully stepping between the sleepers, he made his way to it and lay down.

5
LUNGDREN

JIM LUNGDREN and Acel Stecker sat at a table in the seamen's eating place, "seventy-six." Their table was at a window overlooking the East River. At the dock lay a freighter flying the flag of Spain. The hull was streaked by red lead, and her shore lines gleamed in the morning spring sun like huge watch chains.

Lungdren and Acel had been shipmates. They had encountered each other in the recreation hall of the Seafarers' Home that morning.

Lungdren was a lean, bony-hipped man with a chin like a doorknob. It was covered with a pubescent fuzz. He chewed the sweet roll now with the fearful cautiousness of a man whose teeth are bad. "You don't have any business hanging around a waterfront," he said.

Acel stirred his coffee. "What I want to do is look up that fellow here. I just got a hunch that something might come out of it. He's from my home town, see? If he wanted to he could steer me onto a job as easy as that."

"You're not going to get any place hanging around a waterfront."

"I can't go and see him, looking like a bum."

"I got a couple of bucks if that's what it takes to get that suit out. Don't stand back on that."

"I don't want to take your money. You better hang onto that."

"It's going, anyway. I'll be carrying the banner myself in another week. There's old Boats. Hey, Boats!"

Boats came to their table and placed on it a cup of coffee and three sweet rolls.

"How's the revolution coming along?" Acel said.

"Hello," Boats said. "How did you like your bed last night?"

Lungdren pushed the tin of sugar toward Boats. "I hear you got a ship."

Boats nodded. "I'm shipping Monday. About a four weeks' trip, I guess."

Acel watched Boats's right hand stir the sugar. It was larger than his left and scarred.

"So you got a good sleep in the Hoover Hotel?" Boats said.

"It was okay. I been thinking about putting up in it by the week."

Boats laughed. He broke his sweet roll and then looked at Acel again. "Did you ever read Karl Marx?"

"Uh huh."

"Bernard Shaw?"

"Nope."

"Don't let him horse you," Lungdren said to Boats. "I was shipmates with this guy. He reads all the time. He's had some good jobs, and I been telling him that he——"

"Aw, can that stuff, Lungdren," Acel said.

"If I could play a ukulele I wouldn't be around this part of town," Lungdren said. "Ace is a musician."

"Seamen are not the only ones having a hard time," Boats said. "Say, you two, you want to go up on the Bowery at noon for something to eat? I raised a few nickels this morning."

"There's a joint up there that really feeds," Lungdren said. "Three hunks of ham that thick and enough potatoes for an army, and I don't mean a cup of coffee, but a bowl. And cake. By god, all the cake you can eat. And just for fifteen cents."

Acel looked out the window at the forecastle of the Spanish freighter. On its deck two seamen were chipping rust.

"I don't see how those joints feed like that," Lungdren went on. "You can read in the papers how much it costs to feed a man a bowl of soup in one of those municipal places."

"The cost is in paying the welfare workers to find out whether you're hungry or not," Boats said. "It costs ninety cents for them to get your name and how old you are, and the rest of the dollar goes for food and shelter. What infuriates me is not the relief workers, but the men who are satisfied to stand in soup lines and take whatever is handed them."

"I haven't read Shaw and I haven't read Marx," Acel said, "but I know this Boats that there is a survival-of-the-fittest law. The strong are always going to have more than the weak. I'm sittin' in this dump here, and the reason for it is because I'm not strong enough to be sittin' in Childs'. However, I'll be eatin' in Childs' before it ends."

"Ace has had some good jobs," Lungdren said.

"Ace believes in getting what he can," Boats said.

"It's too big a job," Acel said. "You're not going to reform this world."

"You guys quit your arguing," Lungdren said. "Let's get out of here and go out on the pier. I see some guys over there in swimming."

They descended the narrow stairway to the street. A passenger boat was gliding on the river toward the Sound. Boats left them.

Acel and Lungdren moved toward the Seafarers' Home. "That guy is too radical," Acel said. "These Reds are dopes."

"Aw, don't get old Boats down wrong. He's not any beach scum. That guy has a first-mate's ticket."

"What's the matter with that hand of his?"

"He got it in the navy. He gets a government pension,

thirty bucks a month. He don't feel with that hand. He can cut himself and not even know it."

"I don't have much use for guys that think they know it all."

"He talks a lot, but he's the only one around, just about, that will tell the people that run the Seafarers' what's what. I notice that after he raises a stink they treat us a little better around here. Most of these Communists are dopes, but Boats isn't exactly a Communist. I saw him whip the hell out of two guys right yonder in that park one day. He knocked a guy's ear halfway off with his fist. I mean it, too. That guy's ear was hanging down."

The Seafarers' Home was a fourteen-story corner edifice of steel and brownstone. A uniformed policeman stood near its front entrance and another policeman just inside the lobby. The second policeman halted strangers and demanded the presentation of seamen's papers.

Acel and Lungdren passed on through the lobby and up the stairway to the recreation hall. It was a half-block long and hummed like a running belt with the voices of hundreds of men. Checkers clattered, and through the loud speaker in its center from time to time came the sound of paged names.

At the reading tables sat seamen in the shiny-billed caps of oilers and wipers, and men with the rope-muscled arms of seafarers who work on deck. Men lay face down on the tables, with their heads pillowed on their forearms. Some dozed in chairs or slept boldly on the benches next to the walls. Always there were restless streams of them going in and coming out.

"Boats is always giving this place hell," Lungdren said. "He says this joint is exploiting the seaman and that it's being run for——"

"To hell with Boats," Acel said. He lowered his head to study again the picture of Paul Whiteman in the magazine.

"Aren't you going to take him up on that feed on the Bowery?"

"You can go on with him if you want to. I'm not."

The man approaching the bench on which Acel and Lungdren sat walked with a stiff-kneed, painful gait. He had on a new, tight-fitting suit and brown army shoes. His face looked like a movie muscle man's. He lowered himself carefully to the bench.

"Looks you got a game leg on you," Acel said.

Muscle Man nodded. "Yeah, I just got out of the hospital." He had a growling voice. "Seven months I did. Busted both these legs right across there." He drew a forefinger across his knees.

"Good god, how did you do that?"

Muscle Man said he was standing on a corner, fogbound over a girl, and some gangsters mistook him for an enemy and threw him in front of a truck.

"You look like a dick, all right," Acel said.

"Everybody takes me for a dick or a gangster."

Muscle Man eased off his shoes and exhibited a blood-soaked heel. He said he had got it from walking that afternoon over to Jersey looking for a ship job.

"You want a ship bad enough," Acel said.

"I'll have one pretty soon."

"How do you ship?"

"Like I told that skipper today. I've shipped everything from deck boy to master."

"You been a skipper?"

Muscle Man said he had been the master of a three-sticker. He lost the ship in a fire on the Gulf, but it wasn't the loss of the ship that caused him to lose his officer's papers. It was a missing Filipino that was on the ship. Everybody on the ship was saved except the Filipino. The *goo goo* was the one who fired the ship, Muscle Man said.

"You mean they thought you wouldn't let the *goo goo* go?" Acel said.

"I ain't saying," Muscle Man said.

Lungdren sharpened a match and began cleaning his fingernails.

"Have you ever been in the Orient?" Acel said.

Muscle Man said he had lived in the Far East seven years and had captained a ship for a river pirate queen. He said he had been master of a treasure-hunt ship. There was a volcano lake in South America that was filled with the gold sacrifices of natives. He knew how to drain the lake, and as soon as he got on his feet he was going to raise the finances for another expedition.

Lungdren got up. "Let's go," he said.

Acel told Muscle Man good-bye, and he and Lungdren walked toward the Hoover Hotel.

"There's a man that's sure been around," Acel said.

"That guy was full of blow."

"Those knees weren't full of blow."

"There's plenty of men around here that's been farther than that guy. Boats has been ten times more places than that guy. Boats can talk Chinese."

"He might be bullin' some, but that man has been around. He's not any South Street bum."

They found spots under the boarded window on the fifth floor. Soon Lungdren was snoring, but Acel shifted restlessly and curled in vain in an effort to escape the warped floor board underneath the newspapers.

I turned in too soon, Acel thought. If a man is going to sleep in a place like this he ought to at least wait until he's played out. This time tomorrow I ought to know if I'm going to get any place with Gholson. It's a long shot. No use of kiddin' myself or expecting anything. But a man can't ever tell.

The only way a man ever gets a job is to ask for it. I've asked, haven't I? Yes, but a man has to keep asking. I'm due for a break. If I got a job I could get a girl. If I could get a job in a dance band . . . It's a long shot, though, seeing Gholson.

I should have waited until I was tired. Old Lungdren there is a white man. I'll pay him back that two bucks if it's the last thing I do. That suit of mine won't look bad. These shoes are bad, but I'll get them shined. If I did get a job I'd sure see to it that old Lungdren got a break. I'll come down here dressed up sometime and visit around, and if I'm doing pretty good I'll stake Lungdren to a new suit. I'd like to be jellied out and staking Lungdren and run into Boats. "Well, you started that revolution yet, Boats?"

Muscle Man? Fogbound over a girl and thrown in front of a truck? If that had been me standing there on that corner I'd of jerked away from them. *The truck swerved around the corner and Ace Stecker leaped to safety. There was a jarring crash, and the truck turned over. The gangsters were pinned underneath. A black bag fell at the feet of Ace Stecker. A crowd was gathering. Ace picked up the black bag unobserved and stuffed it underneath his jacket. He walked away and went into the subway station. In the pay toilet he opened the bag. There were stacks of currency held by rubber bands . . .*

The crackle of papers at the entrance of the room disrupted Acel's daydreaming, and he raised up and peered through the darkness. A big, compact figure moved painfully into the room and looked about, searching. Lungdren and me got the last spots, Acel thought.

Acel lay back down and listened to the slow, painful steps of Muscle Man fading on the gritty stairway.

6

GHOLSON

ON THE shawl-draped piano of Red Gholson's studio apartment was a photograph of the orchestra leader in a gold frame. The frame matched the golden rug. Acel, sitting on the piano bench and waiting for Gholson's appearance, decided again not to smoke.

I hope he doesn't smell the gasoline or whatever it is they cleaned this suit of mine with. That's the trouble with four-bit cleaning. At least I can say I met Red Gholson. I can say, "No, I've never met Ben Bernie, but I know Red Gholson. I met him in New York one time." I feel pretty cool waiting to see him. He talked over the telephone like he was a pretty good fellow. . . .

Gholson came in. He looked older than his photographs. He was a small man with red hair, and his face had a Turkish-bath flush. The hand he extended had the diamond on it. Acel had heard Gholson's daddy in Bovina City talk about that diamond. It cost five thousand dollars.

"I'm sorry I kept you waiting," Gholson said.

"That's all right," Acel said.

Gholson sat down in a blue-cushioned chair, and Acel lowered himself to the bench again.

"How is everything in Bovina?" Gholson said.

"Everything was okay when I left there. I haven't been there in a pretty good while myself."

"What's on your mind, Stecker? That is the name, isn't it?"

"Yes. I tell you, Mr. Gholson, I just got in town and I'd like to find a job."

"Are you a musician?"

"Oh, yes. Ten years. I was Wymore's first trumpet for two years and a half, and I had the Apaches at school. You know some of those boys."

"Yes, I know some of those boys." Gholson twisted the diamond on his finger thoughtfully for several moments. "I tell you, Stecker, times are pretty hard here in New York now. Lot of boys out of work now."

Acel nodded. "Yes, I know. I tell you, just any sort of job would put me on my feet."

"You are not particular, then?"

"Oh, no. To tell you the truth, I hoboed it up here. Anything would look good to me."

"Lot of boys are out of work. Some very good boys are out of work now."

"I know things are tough, all right."

Gholson got up. "I tell you what, then. Where are you staying?"

"I'm staying at the Seafarers' Home. It's a pretty reasonable place."

"Well, I'll see if I can't dig you up something. If I hear of anything I'll let you know. You keep in touch with me."

"That sure is nice of you."

"I'll see if I can't dig you up something. You give me a ring in a week or so."

Acel walked down Park Avenue. By god, by god, by god . . .

Lungdren, sitting with his feet over the edge of the pier, shook his head. "No, you don't have nothing to worry about now."

"It's a break, all right," Acel said. "Just a little pull, that's what it takes. A man like him can just put in a word for you, see? and you're sittin' jake. There's jobs, all right. Now you take these excursion-boat musicians. Those fellows get sixty-five bucks a week. I wouldn't know what to do with that much money coming in every week."

"Naw, you ain't got nothing to worry about now."

"I've made more than sixty-five bucks. Listen, when I was eighteen I made that. I had a band on a carnival, and I had a couple of concessions. Ball games. Had a couple of broads running them. One day I cleared forty bucks. I'll bet you think I'm bullin' you."

"I can tell a guy, all right."

"Gholson is really a big shot, see? When I shook hands with him I felt of that ring. I thought, Bud, you got a rock on you worth five thousand bucks and I got subway fare back to the Battery."

"You got a break all right."

"He says to me, 'Give me a ring and let me hear from you.' A big shot like him isn't saying a thing like that unless he means business. And he didn't ask me why I was out of a job or how come me to be in a seamen's place or anything like that."

Lungdren pointed up the pier. "Yonder's the Mad Wolf I was telling you about."

Acel looked at the figure going across the pier in a half-loping walk. His hanging shirt tail napped like a coolie coat, and his trousers bagged like the skin on an elephant's hind legs.

"So that's the Mad Wolf?"

"That's him."

"I wonder if he did lose two thousand dollars in a bank and it made him go crazy."

"That's what they say."

"Don't look to me like that would make a man go crazy."

"If you'd saved it all working below you'd think it was enough, I'll bet."

"I don't know about these loons running around here. I don't know whether they're so crazy or not. I was watching that guy they call Doc up in the Bowery the other day. That one they say went crazy after he operated on a caught girl and she died. I watched him. Every time anybody offered him any money he acted like he was insulted and run off. What does he go around looking like a bum for and mixing around with crowds unless he is a bum? I think he enjoys martyring himself."

"You can't tell me they're not crazy."

The excursion boat rounded the bend from Battery Landing. Holiday flags whipped in the breeze, and a black plume rolled from her high stack. The loaded decks were splashed with the bright-colored figures of women.

Acel and Lungdren stood up as the ship neared. It was so close that they knew now that the girl in the red jacket was waving at them. Another girl beside her focused a camera on them. Acel and then Lungdren waved. The girl in the red jacket waved until the vessel was almost around the bend.

They sat down. "If you'd say anything to one of them on the street they'd call a cop," Lungdren said.

Acel nodded. "I've thought about it when I was on a freight train and some girl would wave at you from a Packard. They'll flirt and wave at you like you were somebody they knew as long as there is plenty of distance between you."

"That's right, all right."

"I know one thing, if I get this job I'm gettin' me a girl the first thing. I'm fed up on this."

"That's what I got against the sea. All you meet is a bunch of whores rollin' you for your dough."

"The last girl I had put me on a wild-goose chase. I was up in Denver, and I got a letter from her. She said I had a good chance for a job in a band she was singing in. I lit out. That was the trip I saw that bum commit suicide on."

"What did he do it for?"

"I don't know. He just jumped out on his head. I'd been riding with him nearly all day. He never had said much, and then that night he just started hopping toward the door like a frog, and then out he went. The train was going like a bat out of hell."

"I wonder what he did it for."

"I don't know. When the train stopped at the next station, my buddy and me told the brakie about it, but they said they couldn't do anything about it. I sure had some tough luck on that trip. We got out of that car and was gettin' in a reefer and I busted this little finger. See the scar here? Damned near took it off. It made me sick as a dog, and my buddy wrapped it up in a handkerchief, and I rode all that night, and the next morning we got in Albuquerque. I put a Catholic hospital there on the bum to dress it up. I was afraid of lockjaw or something. They fixed me up, and I got a train out of there that night for El Paso."

"Where was you eatin'?"

"They fed me in the hospital. One of them sisters gave me a whole bunch of cakes. But I was telling you about gettin' to El Paso. I got booted off that train, and I don't mean just pushed off. The conductor that kicked me off had had a brother killed by a bum just about a week before. He kicked me off in the damnedest town you ever did see. Wasn't nothing but Mexicans there. Well, there was a school teacher and his wife. I hit those Mexicans up, and I couldn't even rate a cigarette. I found out there was a passenger train that stopped there for mail at three in the morning. I had to stay in that place all that afternoon and night until three o'clock next morning. I walked up a road about a mile where these school teachers lived and hallooed and hollered around. I'd waited like a damn fool until after dark. Finally some woman come to the door and said she couldn't do anything, so I started back up the road."

"She didn't give you a thing?"

"She was scared and afraid to open the door, I think.

What was funny, though, was going back. The mosquitoes along the Rio Grande there make those in Galveston look like gnats. I decided I'd better make one of those smudges to keep them off of me. I started looking for cow chips in the road. It was dark, and I got down on my knees and started feeling around. I couldn't even find cow chips in that damned town."

7

THE CAKE LINE

LUNGDREN blew his nose again in the grey handkerchief and then folded it up and stuck it in his hip pocket.

"You ought to try and get some hospital relief, man," Acel said. "You've had that cold long enough."

"My eyes is what bothers me. It's my eyes."

"They'd fix you up with glasses. They would stop that burning."

"There's so much red tape to go through."

Acel got up from the bench and stretched, raising up on his toes. He turned around and placed his foot on the bench. "I think I'll see what I can get on that suit tomorrow. I ought to get three or four bucks. That suit cost me forty-five bucks new without extra pants, either. It's pretty old now, but it isn't worn through any place."

"You better not hock that suit. That Gholson guy might call you yet."

"I've checked that. If he was going to help me get a job he'd have done it long ago. What good does it do for me to phone except cost me a nickel? That stuff about him not being there is all bull."

"You can't expect a job in a couple of weeks."

"It's been four weeks. Man, you oughten to blow your nose that hard. That's the way mastoid trouble gets started."

Lungdren got up. "If we're going to make the Tubes tonight we might as well get started."

They crossed the park and at the corner stopped and watched a razor-blade demonstration. The vendor gesticulated and sprayed spittle like a Socialist in Union Square. He showed how the blue could be scraped off the steel.

They moved on. "That's what I need," Lungdren said. "The next piece of change I get hold of, that's the first thing I'm going to buy. Razor blades."

"I went three weeks one time without shaving at sea," Acel said. "I had a beard that long. I wish I was at sea tonight. I'm going to make the rounds tomorrow again."

"If you had four or five dollars to slip to one of these shipping masters you might could get out," Lungdren said.

"I wish I could get a ship. You know how I'd pass the watches away when I was at sea? I'd skip and shadow-box around the winches. It'd be blowing to beat the dickens some nights, and the lines and the waves hittin' 'midships, and it would all sound like a thousand kettledrums. I'd sing, too. Down the ventilator, every song I could think of."

"I'd rather have a good job ashore."

"I ought to get a ship if I keep on. I'd like to go to the Orient. Did you ever date a Chink girl?"

"Yeah." Lungdren pointed at the bright entrance of the restaurant across the street. "That place is good. I've seen fellows hit it, and they never do get turned down."

"You take that place and I'll take the one right below it," Acel said.

Lungdren shook his head. "I just don't like to do that. You can go on and hit it. It's good."

"That's funny to me, why you won't hit cafés. And you'll stop anybody on the street and bum them for a smoke. I'd just as soon ask a man for a dime as a cigarette."

Acel went across the street and entered the restaurant. Pretty soon he came out and rejoined Lungdren leaning there against the lamppost. "You've seen one guy turned down, anyway. They told me the boss was out and they couldn't do it."

"That must be the reason, then, because I've seen plenty make it. Here, here's a tailor-made. . . . That's all right. I bummed a couple of them."

Acel entered the cafeteria on the corner. It was a glittering place of tile floor and porcelain cases trimmed in shining nickel. The bald cashier looked at him.

"Could I do a little work for something to eat?"

The cashier jerked his head toward the rear.

Acel walked down the bright floor past the long glass cases of food and approached the white-uniformed man behind the counter. "The man up at the desk sent me back," he said.

The counterman went to the kitchen slot and yelled: "A bowl."

The heavy soup was like liquor in Acel's stomach, and he grinned triumphantly as he approached Lungdren. "That was a white place, boy," he said. "You ought to go in there."

"We better be gettin' on down to the Tubes. It's gettin' close to midnight."

The crowds were thinning in the great underground station of the Hudson Tunnels. Here and there in waiting huddles of twos and threes Acel and Lungdren recognized and spoke to the shabby figures of South Street acquaintances.

"They ought not to gang up like that," Lungdren said. "That's what makes the cops sore."

They moved about in the crowd, always hovering near the lunch stand where, at twelve o'clock, the left-over sandwiches and cakes of the day were distributed.

They paused to speak to a seaman called Hunky. He was a short, rotund man with small glassy eyes and a deep cleft in his chin. "We had a pretty good thing here," Hunky said, "until all the damned bums in New York started making this place. There's more here tonight than I ever have seen. Those old smoke belches from the Bowery are gumming it up. They'll make it so pretty soon that it's not worth a man's time to come here any more."

The white-capped counterman began dumping doughnuts and sweet rolls on the counter. Ragged men sifted
quickly through the crowds of commuters, and soon a limp
line of more than fifty bums had formed. The counterman
began handing out two doughnuts to each man.

Commuters halted and stared at the dragging line. Lungdren, in front of Acel, turned and said out of the corner
of his mouth: "The sons of bitches. That's what I hate,
them standing there with their goddamned eyes stickin'
out and watchin'."

The counterman handed Acel one doughnut, and Acel
did not move.

The counterman made a shoving motion with his hand.
"Not enough to go around now."

Acel had to hurry to catch up with Lungdren. The gaunt
seaman, handed a cruller, had walked swiftly away. Acel
found him panting in a shadowed aperture which led behind a big display case.

"I hate them bastards standing out there and looking at
us," he said.

Acel sat down beside him. "That guy they call Hunky. I
don't have any use for a man like him. Griping around as
if this was his own private bumming place. Those Bowery
bums are not walking clear over here for the exercise."

Lungdren bit cautiously on the cruller.

"No, those guys don't deserve anything," Acel said. "There
was one thing about Boats, he was willing to share what he
had. I wonder where that bird is."

"I just can't eat these things." Lungdren's voice had bro-
ken, and he looked helplessly at the dry cake in his hand.
"I just can't eat them. They turn to powder in my mouth."
He swallowed as if his throat were sore.

Acel extended his doughnut. "Maybe you can eat a
doughnut. It's not the same kind of dough."

Lungdren shook his head. "I don't want to take that from
you."

"Ferchrissakes. Go ahead. Here . . . I ate good in that restaurant. You remember. I don't want it, anyway."

"You can have this cruller, then."

They ate silently. Acel listened to the roar of the great station. He brushed sugar off his trouser legs. I'll soak that suit tomorrow. I'll get two or three bucks for it. I'm going to hit every agency and every ship that comes in until I get a ship.

"Say, Lungdren, it'd be pretty nice if we could get a ship together."

Lungdren nodded. "It's funny, ain't it, how we don't work and yet we live?"

8

SHIPMASTER KLOTZ

THERE were not even pictures of women in corsets in the backs of these old magazines—*Farm & Fireside, American Boy, Editor & Publisher*—not even bathing suits. The hairs of Acel's moist forearm clung to the fly-paper varnish of the reading table as he pushed the magazines aside.

Acel looked across the hall. Lungdren was entering, and he stood now looking about searchingly. Acel stood up and waved. Lungdren leveled his finger at Acel like a pistol, jerking his thumb, and then came toward him. The man with him was Boats.

Boats had on a new blue serge suit and a gray felt hat and red tie. "Hello, Ace," he said. "How's the boy?"

"Okay. You look like you stepped out of a bandbox."

"I been working."

"He's going back tomorrow night," Lungdren said. "He's going to treat us to a spaghetti dinner uptown tonight."

"I wish to hell I had a job," Acel said.

"I can put you next to a mess punk's job," Boats said. "On the *Picfair* over in Jersey. It's an excursion boat that runs up the Sound and back every day."

"I never did work in the galleys," Acel said. "I'm not looking particularly for that kind of a job."

Lungdren exhibited two coupons. "I wouldn't have gotten these if I'd of known old Boats was coming in."

Acel frowned. "What did you do, go and get relief tickets? If you do make a trip, you're going to owe this place everything before you get back."

"All you get around this place free is water," Boats said.

"They haven't charged me yet for sittin' in here," Acel said.

"I don't know whether you're getting that free or not, though, when you think about it," Boats said. "You don't get anything around here for nothing. This place is run to give big salaries to executives. You know how much Judge Ross gets? Seven thousand dollars a year to direct this place. And how much does that bird up there get that writes stuff about starving seamen? Five thousand bucks. Five thousand dollars a year he gets for writing to these stuffed shirts, getting them to jerk loose with endowments and contributions. They raise thousands of dollars every year, and they've had millions of dollars given them, and if a seaman comes around here and he doesn't have any money he's out of luck."

"If they can get away with it, they're pretty smart," Acel said.

"I know that a couple of dollars comes out of my pay every trip I make, and they say it goes to this place. I guess, though, that's why I can get credit here."

"Are you telling me, Ace," Boats said, "that you think it is just for these men that run this place to get big salaries and four hundred seamen sleeping every night over there in the Hoover Hotel?"

"You can't do anything about it, Boats."

"That isn't the question. It's okay, you say, for them to pay themselves seven thousand and five thousand dollars a year and hire cops around here who don't know a half-hitch from a chain-locker. At least they could hire a few seamen around a place like this. The only seamen working around this place are in the galleys. Look, Lungdren, did you ever get anything around here for nothing? Did you ever sleep in this place and not pay for it? Did they ever give you a single meal? You've needed them, haven't you? So have I, but it would do me a helluva lot of good to ask for it. No, this place is to provide seven thousand dollars a year for Judge Ross and some of his women around here. Seven thousand dollars a year. Why, godamighty, the dictator of Russia only gets two hundred and fifty bucks a month, and he runs a nation of one hundred and sixty million people. And that old belch up there gets seven thousand a year, and there are three thousand seamen sleeping every night on the streets or in flop houses or half-burned buildings like the Hoover Hotel."

"Get you a soap box," Acel said.

"You're no seaman, though, I forget," Boats said. "You're just a vacuum-headed horn blower who got kicked out of his own racket and is hanging around a waterfront now."

Acel got up. "Listen, bud, you don't talk to me——"

"Don't take things too seriously, Ace," Boats said.

"You guys quit your damned arguing," Lungdren said. "You act like a couple of punk. Ferchrissakes."

"You're a long ways from not having a head on you, Ace. That's why you make me so mad. If we men down here struggling in this kind of life can't see the injustice of the capitalistic system, then even a god wouldn't help us."

"I don't see that you have any kick coming," Acel said. "You've got a job, and you got you a good suit and some money to spend. What do you have to gripe about?"

"Christ, man, don't you believe in social equality? Don't you think every man is entitled to food and clothing and shelter? Do you approve of a system that operates so one man can have enough to buy a billion meals and another can't raise the price of one?"

"Like I've told you before, this is a dog-eat-dog world, and if I don't get mine I'm not going to whine."

Boats knocked the ashes out of his pipe into the spittoon.

"I got to go see about some gear. I'll see you boys down in the lobby about six. You two need tobacco money?"

Acel shook his head.

They watched Boats walk across the hall and disappear on the stairway.

"Are we going around to any shipping agencies this afternoon?" Lungdren said.

"I'm tired of sittin' around those places."

"I heard below a while ago there was a couple of tankers in, and there might be something doing around at Klotz'."

Klotz was head of the Forecastle Shipping Agency. He stood now in the doorway of his office at the end of the long, bare hall. He was in his undershirt, and the belt around his fat stomach was loosened. Under his arm was a bright can.

The benches on the sides of the hall were sprinkled with men. There was a big blackboard on which were printed sea occupations, but the spaces for openings were blank. There was one unoccupied bench, a broken plank, and Acel and Lungdren seated themselves carefully.

Klotz came over to them. His eyes were glassy with drink. He extended the can. "Have a drink," he said.

The beer was tepid and flat. "Thanks, Klotz," Acel said. "Got any jobs around here today?"

Klotz did not answer. He turned and went across the room and stood before a long-jawed seaman in a straw hat.

"Hi, Lantern Jaw," Klotz said.

Lantern Jaw smiled uncertainly.

Klotz reached out and brought back the man's hat. He held it for a moment and then dropped it on the floor. The hat made a crackling sound as he stomped on it, and men in the room laughed.

Lantern Jaw's lips twisted vaguely.

Klotz returned to his office and closed the door.

"Playful today, isn't he?" Acel said.

"The son of a bitch," Lungdren said.

"I don't see much use hanging around this place."

"They shipped a couple of wipers out of here yesterday after we left."

Lungdren got up, and Acel followed him. They descended the stairs and crossed the street and went out on the cement pier. Muscular youths in underwear were running around on the docks and diving into the river.

"Didn't you say you had some folks in Detroit?" Acel said.

"I got a dad and a sister and a brother. I guess they're still there."

"If I had a home I believe I'd go to it."

"I wouldn't go home now. I kept thinking I'd go back home some Christmas with some money, but I don't know, one thing and another come up. I wouldn't go back like I am now for nothing."

"If my aunt hadn't married I probably would be in Bovina now. My aunt raised me, see? She didn't marry until she was forty."

"If I could make a pretty good trip and get a hundred dollars together I wouldn't mind going home. I got a bud. He's twenty-two now. He was eighteen the last time I saw him."

"Don't you ever write to them?"

"Not any more."

"Postcards are about all I write. I haven't written one of them in a long time. When I go to a new place I usually send a few."

Across the river the flags on the two American freighters fluttered violently in the wind. The sounds of winches and booms came across the water.

"I wonder if Boats was on the level about that mess job over in Jersey," Acel said.

"Yeah. Boats wouldn't bull you."

"No, I don't guess he'd bull you about a thing like that."

"Naw, he wouldn't kid you about a thing like that."

9
A DOLLAR A DAY

ACEL descended the steep companionway into the galleys of the S.S. *Picfair*. The heat came up around him like steam. A small, wizened man in silk undershirt and carpet slippers turned from a simmering pot he was stirring on the big army range. The tattooing on his soggy flesh was faded.

"I'm looking for the steward," Acel said.

"I'm him." The steward wiped the front and back of his hand on his soiled white trousers. "I'm the steward."

"I hear you need a messman."

The steward showed teeth like rusty nail heads in a smile. "You get long hours on here."

"That's okay with me. I been on the beach so long that anything looks good to me."

A dark-skinned youth in white trousers and cotton undershirt came down the companionway with a hunk of ice in his hands. Sweat made his long, knotty muscles shine.

"Joe, here's a new messman. Show him around."

In the forward part of the galleys was the officers' mess with a heavy, oilclothed table and twelve swivel chairs. A locker through which the steering gear ran from the pilot house above separated it from the crew's mess near the stove. The crew's table was bare and grey with the streaks of scrubbing brushes and rimmed by folding chairs. There were three portholes on both sides of the galleys, but only the two forward holes were open. Joe said this was because the wash of other ships sometimes flooded the forecastle.

The sink was at the left of the stove. Dish water was heated by a steam pipe which made a deafening, terrifying noise when it was turned on. The water was pumped out by hand.

"This is where you'll get lots of work," Joe said. The sink was filled with pots. "But I get up first in the mornings and make the fires."

Acel stripped to his undershirt and started on the pots. After a while the gangplank thudded on the deck above, and pretty soon the ship began to quiver as the screw turned. Sweat slid off Acel's nose into the sink. He got the steel wool and rubbed vigorously the black-crusted bottom of the pot.

When Acel hung up the last pot and placed the rags over the hot steam pipe, Joe came over. "How you like galley work?" he said.

Acel brought out his tobacco. "I don't mind. I always worked on deck, though. This is my first time in the galleys, between you and me. I've worked in kitchens, though."

"Deckhands get sixty a month on this boat," Joe said.

"One thing about working in the galleys, you get plenty to eat. That's something."

"This boat feeds good."

"The steward is a guiney, isn't he?"

Joe nodded. "He's a good fellow, that guy is. He'll give you the shirt off his back. He owes me about twenty dollars now I been lettin' him have along, but he'll pay it back. People are all the time taking advantage of him, especially women."

"Yeah?"

"He never has a cent after pay day. He'll pay me that, though."

"I'm going to save the money I make on here. I'm sure not going to spend any." Acel dropped his cigarette in the slop bucket.

Joe reached up and rearranged the cloths Acel had hung. "This wouldn't be such a bad job only the hours are pretty long. That's why a lot of these fellows quit."

" 'Bout how long do you have to work on here?"

"I get up at five, but you don't have to get up until five-thirty. Then every other night one of us has to put out the night lunch for the crew."

· "Night lunch on an excursion boat?"

"Yeah. We don't tie up until around nine o'clock at nights. I usually find time in the afternoons to get an hour or so sleep. If you ever want to go ashore to get something when we're at the battery, you can get off for ten or fifteen minutes."

"And every other night one of us has to work later than nine o'clock?"

"Not much to it. Just set out a lunch for the deck and black gangs. Just see to it that they don't get in the ice-box."

"That's a helluva lot of work for a dollar a day, though."

"They don't care on here whether you stay or not. The steward will tell you himself he don't blame a man for quitting."

"Well, I got to save some money."

"I can't be independent like you fellows. I got a mother and sister I got to help. Say, you don't have to fool with the officers' mess. All you got to do is handle the crew's table, see?—but I split the tips with you off the officers. I got a dollar and a quarter last pay day."

The steward came back to the stove. "You fellows better get started on the tables," he said.

Acel started setting the crew's table. He placed the soup spoons alongside the forks, but Joe came and placed them in front of the bowls. He said he had been doing it that way.

There's one thing about long hours, Acel thought, I won't get to go ashore and blow any money. I'm saving my money. I'm going to keep on smoking Bull, too. I won't draw my pay. Just enough for tobacco, and I can get some razor blades. I'd like to get a hundred dollars. If I work the rest of the summer I can do it. With a hundred bucks I could get a new suit and new shoes and have fifty bucks in my pocket. With a new suit and everything and money in my pocket I'd feel different. That is what has been the matter with me. It's psychological. A man can't get a job looking like a bum or feeling like one. I'll see Gholson again. I should never have went to see him in those shoes. . . .

Acel looked around the mopped, shining galleys and then remembered he had not filled the coal scuttles. It was around eleven o'clock. He started filling the scuttles when Joe came in. Joe was dressed up in a brown suit with red stripes. He said the Ken Maynard picture he had seen was good. "You got to hack slivers out of those boxes over there for the fire in the morning, you remember. You'll get through quicker as soon as you get onto things around here a little better."

While Joe was changing clothes, Acel hacked up the box. He swept the splinters into a pan and brushed them in the stove. Joe came over and said the next time Acel should make the slivers smaller.

"How many men have had this job of mine since you been on here?" Acel said.

"I've been on here two months now, and you're the seventh. Naw, eighth, that's it."

"They just quit, uh?"

"Well, one of them was sent uptown by the purser with forty bucks to buy some stuff for the ship, and he just didn't come back."

"I don't much blame them for quittin' around here."

"I can't be independent like you fellows. Don't say anything about it, see? but the purser told me he was going to get me in the cafeteria the first opening. Don't say anything about that."

"Seven quit this job since you been here, uh?" Acel looked toward the thin bunks. "What I hate is the idea of sleeping down here in this sweat box. A man isn't going to rest very well in this."

"I take my mattress up on deck some nights.—Whatsamatter, you got a splinter in your hand?"

Acel quit squeezing his thumb. "By god, can you sleep up on deck? I didn't know they would let you do that. I'm going to stay on this boat until I save some dough. That's all there is to it."

1O

NIGHT LUNCH

MESS PERIODS rushed swiftly for Acel on the S.S. *Picfair*. When Joe went up the companionway to ring the bell, Acel gave the tables a last onceover to see that everything was in place: the catsup and mustard, the salt and pepper, the plates of butter chips at both ends of the table, and the can of condensed milk punched twice with an ice pick.

As the steward filled the soup bowls, Acel would carry them to the table. The crew made a great stomping as they came down the companionway. By the time the first man finished his soup, Acel would be waiting with the big platter of hot meat. He had to see to it that all the platters, the potatoes and gravy and greens, kept moving. There was the pitcher of iced tea that had to be kept filled, too; and, for the men who asked for it, coffee. It was a sort of game to keep someone from yelling for something. If somebody yelled, the steward would rush over: "Whatsamatter? . . . No potatoes. Goddam. They haven't got nothing else to do but wait tables, and I got to cook and wait both."

The steward never yelled directly at Acel. He would curse Joe, though. "Goddamit, you got lead in your pratt. If you can't do this work, say so and I'll get somebody that can."

The crew was discouraged from lingering at the table after dessert. Their dishes were jerked away as soon as they had eaten. This was because there were two other set-ups at the noon period, one for the relief gang and the other for the orchestra. After the three set-ups, Joe, Acel, and Steward ate.

Steward would be solicitous of his messmen when they were alone. "You boys are not eatin' much today. Maybe you want to cook yourself some eggs?"

Joe drank his milk out of a coffee mug.

"I couldn't drink milk that way," Acel said.

"It don't have much taste to it this way, but I drink it like this, see? because they don't know but what I'm drinking coffee, and what they don't know don't hurt them."

"The boss wanted to know yesterday if you boys were feelin' bad," Steward said. "He saw you lying there on your bunks. I told him you boys were hard workers and I don't blame you two for sittin' down whenever you get a chance, but you know how bosses are."

"Yeah, we better watch it, I guess," Joe said.

It was Acel's job, every evening after the supper dishes were washed, to go above and back aft to the cafeteria and get two pitchers of milk for the breakfast cereals. He would wet his hair under the sink faucet, comb it carefully by the cracked mirror over the steward's bunk, and put on clean white trousers and jacket.

If the countermen in the cafeteria were busy this gave Acel a chance to stay on deck awhile. At this time of day the boat would be nearing Hell Gate.

Acel leaned over the rail and watched the shore line and river crafts. The breeze tingled in the roots of his wet hair. They passed another excursion boat, and passengers on both ships waved. A motor launch skimmed astern. Astraddle its bow was a tanned girl in a white bathing suit. She looked like a picture in a movie magazine. Convalescents of the County Hospital stood on the shore in bathrobes and waved. Acel waved at them.

The counterman yelled that the pitchers were filled, but Acel lingered to gaze at the solid masonry and human-specked streets of Manhattan's shore line.

After the boat berthed at its Jersey dock, the black gang

came down into the galleys for a night lunch of cold tongue and cheese and left-over cafeteria sandwiches. The black gang were pallid-skinned, and they did not eat as much as the deckhands, who were making a big clatter at this time stacking chairs and washing the decks above.

After the black gang cleared out, Acel wiped the crumbs off the table and put away the meats and butter in the icebox. Both the steward and Joe were ashore. The boy who came every evening selling Manhattan tabloids came in. Acel bought a tabloid and gave the boy a piece of cake. Feeding the boy made him think of Lungdren. He had left word for Lungdren on the bulletin board of the Seafarers' Home, but the other had never showed up.

Acel did not mind if the deckhands lingered at the table after the night lunch, particularly the Armenian deckhand, Kasha. The Armenian was a broad, wrestler-muscled sea-man who could lift up one side of the gangplank single-handed. He gave Acel a book on Socialism by Bernard Shaw. He said he had bought the book, but he had thrown his money away because he couldn't read it.

Tonight, after the other deckhands had gone above to play poker, Kasha said: "Did you read any of that book today?"

Acel shook his head. "No, I didn't find any time today."

"I was thinking about what you said yesterday," Kasha said. "About men who won't work ought to be killed whether he's a bum or a rich man with a million dollars. I believe in that."

"That book says that it takes nine men working hard to support a tenth man in wealth, and it's this tenth man who ought to get it in the neck. I guess it means that when times are hard the tenth man can't use but five or six men and the rest have to bum."

"And they do their bummin' off the five or six men who are working for the rich men," Kasha said.

"That's right."

"And if these three or four men out of a job kick about it, the tenth man gets the five or six working for him to whip them."

Acel nodded. "You got it figured out right. That's the way it is. The police work for the rich."

Joe came in with a shirt he had gotten at the Chinese laundry. "The steward is up the street drinking three two," he said.

"If he's drinking I'll bet you have a hard time gettin' him up in the morning again," Acel said.

"I saw a couple of bums have a fight up the street," Joe said. "The little bum threw a rock at the big one, and it hit a restaurant front and the glass fell down on the big guy. The side of his face hung down on his shoulder. It made me sick at my stomach."

"He must have been canned up," Kasha said.

"Yeah, he was. Both of them."

"Did you-all ever hear about those Chinks in that chain locker out on the West Coast? . . . That's the bloodiest thing I ever heard about. Some mate was smuggling Chinks over here, and he'd put them in the chain locker, and when everybody else went ashore he'd slip forward and let them out. He got a hundred dollars a head, I think. One time, though, the ship had to anchor out before they could tie up. He had about six Chinks in that hole, and he was sweating. If he went ahead and let them drop the anchor, those Chinks would come out of that hawser hole in chunks, and if he told the skipper, it meant prison for him."

"What did he do?" Joe said.

"The Chinks went out in chunks."

11

STEWARD

ACEL'S new suit was a tweed with patch pockets and broad, peaked lapels. It cost fourteen dollars and ninety-five cents. There was a new shirt, too, blue, and a dark blue tie and socks and underwear, all bought in the five, twenty-five, and one-dollar store. The canvas beach bag with a zipper and an orange-and-chocolate stripe around it was the bargain. It cost ninety-eight cents. A man could highway or grab a moving train with it. The extravagance was the shoes, black-and-white oxfords. A bum with white shoes? They weighed on his mind.

He kept the new clothes under the curtains by his bunk, and for a while he worried a good deal about the possibility of having them stolen. He would part the curtains several times a day and make sure they were still there. But it would be pretty hard for somebody to get them, because he was in the galleys nearly all the time, and if he went ashore he would wear them.

I have a good front now. Lungdren won't recognize me in that rig-out. I can have those shoes dyed black this fall, and if I stay on here thirty more days I'll have fifty bucks. I got twenty coming to me now, and when I get the fifty I'm ready to shove off. If a man can't get places with a good front and fifty bucks he might as well quit. I'll see Gholson, and this time I will ask him to suggest some men

I can see. If I can go to them and mention that Gholson suggested it, I'll get places. I can do it with a good front and staying at a "Y" and not worrying about where I'm going to put the bing on somebody next. I can look like somebody now.

Joe was having a hard time getting the steward up this morning. It was seven o'clock, and Acel had the breakfast set-up on and the cereals ready.

Joe shook the steward again. "Aw right, Steward, you'd better get up. It's after seven o'clock, Steward. You better get up now."

The steward made a croaking sound and pretty soon was snoring again. Joe kept going back.

"Ferchrissakes, let him lay there," Acel said.

The steward finally got up. His face looked like a bacon rind, and his hangover breath was rancid. He went over to Joe. "Who told you to put that bacon in the stove?" he said.

"I just thought I'd do it."

"Am I the steward on here or you? You're meddlin' all the time. Meddlin'. *Meddlin'!*"

"I just thought I'd do it for you."

"Who told you to? You're not responsible for breakfast. If they don't like it on here, they can fire me. It's none of your goddamned business."

"Aw right, Steward."

"It's none of your goddamned business."

"Aw right, Steward. Aw right."

After breakfast they made turkey sandwiches. This was Sunday, and the excursion-boat crowds were big. It was Acel's job to smear melted butter on the slices of white bread and pass them to the steward, who sliced the turkey and patted the meat on the bread. Joe wrapped the sandwiches in waxed papers.

Sweat dripped from their foreheads. Joe went out and tried to get some beer for the steward, but the Sunday-closing law made him return empty-handed. The steward muttered as he sliced the meat.

"Folks ought to like these four-bit sandwiches," Acel said. "They're sweat-flavored."

The steward straightened. "We're clean down here."

"The hell we are!" Acel said.

After that they worked silently.

At noon the steward was solicitous of the crew as they ate. He waited on them himself. He stood at the table, a towel around his neck, and complained about Joe. "If they like him better than they do me, they can fire me, but I'm the steward on here now and he's just a smart guy. That's what he is, smart guy. I try to be a good guy, and in my heart I know I'm a good guy, but I'm not going to stand for any two-facin', and if they like him better than they do me, they can just tell me and I'll get out and they can have him."

Acel was washing dishes when the steward yelled at him. The steward pointed at Kasha. "Coffee for this man," he said.

Acel lifted another plate out of the hot water and placed it on the drainboard. Then he dried his hands.

"I'm the steward on here, and it's none of his damned business whether this ship eats or not, and if he keeps on, either me or him is going. They can decide between us, because I'll fire him off of here if he don't snap out of it, and that goes for you, too, *big boy!*"

Acel lowered the cup of coffee on the table beside Kasha's plate. When he looked up, the steward was shaking his finger. "I mean *you*, too!"

"I quit this job," Acel said. He began undoing his apron.

"You betcha you quit. Tonight you're finished."

"I'm finished now."

"No, you're not finished now."

Acel went over and threw his apron on the bunk. He pulled a towel down off the pipe and began wiping his face.

The steward approached him. "You're not going to quit now."

"You go to hell, you goddamned guiney."

The steward jerked forward, stopped, and strained as if on a leash. Kasha looked at Acel and made a spiraling motion with his finger against his head and pointed at the steward. Acel's right hand hung loosely. The steward suddenly looked drained. Acel turned and began taking off his undershirt.

After he had arranged his new clothes on the bunk and crammed his working gear in the zipper bag, Acel filled the galvanized iron bucket and began to shave. The steward went over and began to help Joe wash the dishes.

"I quit that job down there," Acel announced to the purser.

The purser nodded.

"I'm going to stay up here on deck, and if you want to charge me like a passenger you can take it out of my pay tonight when we get back to Jersey."

"That's all right," the purser said.

Acel bought a package of tailor-mades in the cafeteria. After that he went over to the saloon where a half-dozen couples were dancing to the ship's orchestra. After watching them awhile he went up on the top deck and walked forward and sat down on the lifeboat cradle behind the pilot house.

Twenty bucks I got coming. Twenty bucks and a half really, but I won't get paid for this morning. Twenty bucks? I can last a long time on that. I can carry the banner three or four nights a week and every week-end get a six-bit room at the Seafarers' and clean up. I can last a long time that way. Times are picking up. This N.R.A. Ships are coming out of the boneyards. Russia. Plenty of cotton freighters will move this fall.

Two girls sat on chairs next to the rail diagonally from

Acel. The one with the orange scarf around her neck faced Acel. Her feet rested on the chair of the other, and her candy-striped skirt lay parted high on her slightly opened knees. Acel looked at Orange Scarf's knees. She brushed the skirt down a little.

The other girl had on a plaid gingham blouse. She said, "D.D.R.," and Orange Scarf put her finger to her forehead thoughtfully and in a moment said, "Dolores Del Rio."

After a while Orange Scarf looked at Acel and smiled. "Would you like to play movies with us?" The girl in the blouse turned and looked at Acel.

Acel shook his head. "I'm afraid I wouldn't be much good at that game."

They went on playing the game.

I should have went over there, Acel thought. I had a good chance to get in with them. But what could I do with a couple of girls? Get stuck for sandwiches and beer. I see myself puttin' out for beer, and me with the beach staring me in the face again. I'd just be chump enough, though, to do it if I went over there. I don't have any money to blow on women.

Acel got up and walked toward the pilot house. Before he turned he looked back. Orange Scarf was watching, but she lowered her head. Acel walked on, and his heels clicked on the deck.

Kasha turned from the flag line he was tying. "I didn't know you in that rig-out. Well, what do you say?"

"Everything is okay with me."

"That steward is screwy," Kasha said.

"I got a bellyful of it. If I'd of stayed there much longer I would have had to take a punch at him or something."

"They told me in the cafeteria to tell you that if you got hungry they'd fix you up."

"That's white of them. Yeah, I just got a bellyful of it down there with that steward."

"What are you going to do now?" Kasha said. "You going to be around the Seafarers'?"

"I guess I'll go down there. I got a few bucks, though, and I'm not worrying. Maybe we can be shipmates again sometime."

Acel went back to the saloon and leaned through the window beside the orchestra. When the dance ended, the fat saxophone player got up and stood beside him.

"I used to play in bands," Acel said.

"That's what one of the boys was telling me."

"You-all got a pretty nice band here."

"Thanks. Why don't you dance? There's plenty of good-looking women on this boat today. Why don't you tie into one?"

"I been thinking about it."

"The next number is a waltz."

"I been thinking about it, all right."

A girl in a white linen suit holding the hand of a child in a sailor's blouse came out of the saloon and took seats beside two older women. The girl was not much larger than the child. The light brown curls under her cocked béret looked soft and fresh.

Acel kept looking at Soft Curls. Now that's something. I could go for a girl like that. Baby, you're the prettiest thing on this boat. I could marry a girl like that. You are exquisite, baby. That's the word for you. *Exquisite*. Will you dance with me? May I have this dance with you? You're the prettiest thing on this boat. . . .

The waltz began. Acel went over and stood above Soft Curls. "Would you dance?"

Soft Curls smiled and got up. The two older women smiled. Acel's hand trembled on her back as they entered the saloon.

The floor was like cork, and the music seemed noisy. Acel winked at the fat saxophone player. "Do you live in New York?" Soft Curls said.

Acel lessened the pressure of his hand on her back. "No, I live in California."

"California. My, you are a long ways from home."

"It's a pretty good piece, all right. Do you like this step all right? I saw it first in Denver. I like waltz rhythm, don't you?"

"I don't dance much on account of my operation."

"Have you had an operation?"

"This is about the first time I have danced since I had my operation."

A couple bumped into them, and Acel apologized.

"You don't look like a girl that's been sick. I looked at you a long time before I asked you to dance. I was thinking that you're the prettiest thing on this boat."

"What did you say? I did not understand you."

"I say you don't look like you've been sick."

"Mama says I shouldn't dance at all, because it is too soon after my operation. That's my mother yonder and my aunt."

"How about the next dance? I'd like to sew it up, because there's more fellows on here with their eyes on you, and it's not safe to wait until the last moment."

"I don't think so. Mama will just have a fit now because I've only been out of the hospital five weeks. I can't dance too much."

Acel escorted her back to the older women and then went over and leaned through the window by the fat saxophone player.

"You know how to pick them, all right," the musician said.

"She wasn't so bad."

A slender girl with a grey tunic coat on her arm stood in the doorway on the other side of the saloon. A pancake hat tilted forward over her right eye. She had a long nose and a dark complexion. As soon as the music started, Acel approached her.

She shook her head.

"Why, don't you dance?" Acel said.

"Not very much."

"I'll bet you do. I wish you would."

"I don't dance very well."

"Come on, let's dance."

"But I have this coat here."

"You let me have that and I'll go check it. I'll go check it for you."

She handed him the coat.

Kasha was standing at the checkroom with the first officer. He grinned. "Say, how do you do it?"

"Did you see me? You haven't seen this last one, though. I got one now."

"You got to let me in on how you do it," Kasha said.

"Boy, it's a secret."

After they danced they went up on the cool top deck, and Acel got folding chairs and arranged them on the port side distant from other passengers. The breeze ruffled the silk over her breasts.

"I told you I couldn't dance," she said.

"Shoot, you dance keen. That floor up there isn't so hot, and that band could be a lot better."

She touched her chin. "I wish I didn't have these hickeys on my face."

"You got one of those? I didn't even notice."

They looked across the waters. A horizon of sea crawled against a blue sky. Wind-driven white clouds raced before a smoky blob that seemed to pursue them.

After a while she said her name was Corinne and she had been up in Connecticut visiting an aunt.

"I thought you were turning me down flat, Corinne, when I asked you to dance. I was about to give up. I didn't feel so hot there for a moment."

"I thought you were being fresh when you said, 'Don't you dance?' I told myself I'll just show this fellow I can dance."

Kasha went by and winked.

"Everyone on this boat seems to know you," Corinne said.

"I've been working on this boat. I just quit at noon."

"What did you do on here?"

"I worked on deck."

"You're not going to work on here any more?"

"No, I quit. I took a poke at a fellow and quit."

"It must be fascinating to work on a boat."

"This isn't my line. I've just been doing this to get by for a while. It isn't so bad, though, if you're on a ship that is going some place like Europe, but this river stuff is no good."

"Have you been to Europe?"

"Sure. More than once. My game is music, though. I've played in some good bands. That's the racket I'm getting back into just as soon as things pick up."

"Maybe this N.R.A. is going to help us."

"I hope it does."

Corinne nodded. "I hope it does, too."

After a while Corinne opened her handbag and brought out some kodak pictures. "These are some pictures we made up in Connecticut. Would you like to see them?"

"If you are in them I do."

There was a picture of Corinne in a bathing suit. Her hips curved voluptuously under the skirtless garment. A youth in slacks and sweat shirt stood there with his arm around her.

"That's a boy I ran around with some while I was up there."

"I don't like that part of the picture."

"I got a silly grin on my face."

"I don't call that silly. If you want me to talk plain, that picture is hot. That suit kind of fits you. Looking at that makes me feel funny inside. Honey, I'm tellin' you."

"You are just saying that."

"Don't think I'm just sayin' it. Already I know meeting you isn't going to do me any good. No kiddin', that's a knockout. That suit kind of sets you off."

"You are only saying that. I know that I am skinny."

"The only thing I don't like about this picture is this guy here. He looks like he thinks he's with Miss God or somebody."

"He's just a boy I ran around with some up there."

"You're not sweet on him?"

"Lord, no. He's just a boy I knew up there."

"I'm glad to hear that. No kiddin', sweet, I'm beginning to feel sorry I met you. I was getting along pretty good without a girl, and then one like you comes along and makes me wish I had one. I'm sorry I met you, because now I'll think about you. That's the trouble with you, honey, you're too sweet."

"You are sweet yourself."

Corinne lived in Brooklyn with two unmarried aunts, she said. She was a typist, but she had not worked in more than a year now. Her aunts worked in a department store and threw it up to her at times that she did not act like she wanted to work. "They are awful narrow-minded," she said.

"Yeah, I know," Acel said.

"I hate to go back."

"You had much experience, honey?"

"Sure."

"I mean, you know the kind of experience I mean?"

"Sure."

"I mean sex experience."

"Sure."

Acel pulled out cigarettes, and Corinne took one. The match he held for her trembled. "That's what you are doing to me," he said. "I'm falling for you, honey."

"You certainly are different."

"I'll bet you got a kick out of me choking up the way I did when I asked you if you ever had any experience. I didn't know but what you taught a Sunday school somewhere. I'll bet you got a kick out of that."

"You are sweet."

"I'm gettin' fogbound over you, if you want to know."

Acel flipped his cigarette high in the air and watched its breeze-tossed spiral to the water. "I guess your aunts will be waiting for you at the Battery?"

"Lord, no. They don't know when I'm coming in for sure. I wrote and told them I would be home yesterday, but they don't know."

"They don't know when you'll be in, then, for sure?"

Corinne shook her head. "They'll complain whenever it is. I know them."

"Let's make it tomorrow then?"

"I don't know what you mean."

"I mean that tonight you and I will be together."

"Oh, I can't do that."

"What's to keep you from it?"

"Oh, I couldn't do that. I'm in bad enough at home now. Besides, where would we go?"

"Don't you worry about that. We'll find a place to go."

"No, I can't do that."

"Why not, honey? You can't let me down now. I'm too far gone on you. I don't want to tell you good-bye down at the Battery. C'mon, honey. Say yes. Say it."

"I can give you my address."

"Aw, we're together now, and why can't we just keep on? Aw, don't now. Say yes."

"I really shouldn't."

"Gee, honey, that's the way. That's a break. It's such a break I'm afraid there's a catch in it. Is there a catch in it, baby?"

"I really shouldn't be going with you."

12

CORINNE

BAREFOOTED deckhands worked furiously, stripping the chair-littered decks of the darkened, tied-up S.S. *Picfair*. Acel, with the canvas bag at his feet, waited for the purser. Kasha, chairs under his arms and with his trousers rolled up on his muscular thighs, stopped.

"Where did the girl friend go?"

"She's over in the Lackawanna station."

"She going to cost you much?"

"This is on the level, Kasha. She's nice."

"Oh. Well, I guess I'll see you around the Seafarers' this fall. I guess I'll stay on here until she ties up this fall."

"Sure, we'll see each other."

The purser called through the grilled window of his cabin. He spread the bills out and pushed them under the grill. "Twenty-one dollars. That is right?"

Acel nodded. "Thanks."

The steward, in his apron, leaned in the galleys companionway. When Acel started for the gangplank, he said, "Well, so long, Steward."

The steward approached eagerly. "I told them to pay you for today, a full day."

"That was white of you."

"I'm sorry we couldn't get along."

"I am too, Steward. So long."

Corinne was not in the railroad station. It was a big station, high-vaulted and full of deep-toned echoes. There were not many people on the long, glistening benches. Acel looked over all the benches twice and then went over to the ferry station.

The ferry ticket agent said he hadn't noticed a girl in a pancake hat carrying a week-end bag, but Acel could go in and look around.

She was not in the ferry station.

Acel came out and set his bag on the sidewalk close to the curb. He shook his head at the cab driver. Sweat dripped off his nose, and he wiped his face with his hand and threw off the sweat with a click of his two fingers. He took off his coat and rolled up his sleeves. I don't believe that girl ran out on me. That's the kind of breaks I get, though. A dollar on my pay I wasn't expecting, and now the damned girl gone. It's the best thing, though. I got twenty-one bucks, and it's going to have to last me a long time. I'm pretty good, thinking about blowing money in for hotel rooms with the beach staring me in the face. I would have spent it, too. . . .

He went back into the Lackawanna station.

There she was!

"God, I been lookin' everywhere for you. Where have you been?"

"I was in the rest room. I thought you would be a long time on the boat."

Acel sat down on the bench beside her. "I'm hot as hell."

"You sure are perspiring."

"I'm hot as hell if anybody wants to know."

They lighted cigarettes. "What do you think of us staying over on this side tonight and going on over to New York in the morning?" Acel said.

"If you want to."

He got up and picked up their bags. "Let's get in the saddle, then."

Shadowed fire escapes cobwebbed the rust-colored stone of the waterfront hotel. Acel gave the cab driver a dime tip. They entered the hotel, and Corinne sat in a chair by the elevator, and Acel went up to the clerk with the black sleeve bands.

"How much?" Acel said.

"Five dollars for a double."

"You saw me coming, didn't you, mister?"

"I got one with shower. Four dollars."

Acel picked up the pen. "That's better."

They followed the clerk through narrow, carpeted passageways. Acel grasped Corinne's hand and pressed it. "You got to strike a match to see the light in this hall." Corinne pressed his hand.

They were alone in the room now. Acel looked at the print of a ship at sea on the wall. "This isn't so bad," he said when he turned around.

Corinne sat on the edge of the bed. She shook her head.

"They tried to stick us five bucks for it, though."

"You can stay in uptown New York hotels for that," Corinne said.

"Four dollars isn't so bad, though." Acel slapped his hands. "Can you hold the fort down while I go out and see about a little drinking liquor?"

Corinne stood up and took off her coat. "If you won't be gone too long."

A man at the corner told Acel he could buy gin in three places in that block.

Acel bought a drink at the bar and then two bottles of gin. The gin was seventy-five cents a bottle. He bought two bottles of ginger ale and two lemons and a container of ice.

Corinne was in pajamas. They were blue silk and wrinkled. She sat on the bed with her back against arranged pillows. The humming fan on the wall made the damp curls on her forehead tremble.

Acel placed the sacks on the dresser. "The old man below gave me a lecture," he said. "He said young fellows didn't know when to stop drinking. I told him not to worry, I wasn't going to raise hell. Baby, you look mighty sweet and cool there."

"Did you stop at the drugstore?" Corinne asked.

"Drugstore?"

"You know."

"Dern, I forgot that. Well, I forgot to get cigarettes, anyway, and I got to bum old Sour Face below for another glass. Hold the joint down again, will you, honey?"

When he returned, Acel took a shower. He toweled himself until his skin glowed and came out of the bathroom, bare to the waist. He flexed his arm muscles. "How you like these, baby?"

The surface of the dresser was an untidy miscellany with the gin bottles and cigarettes and Corinne's opened handbag. There was her lipstick and her comb with hairs clinging to it.

Acel took the cork out of the bottle again. "You about ready for another shot?"

"I have been ready."

"We ought to be gettin' a buzz on this stuff pretty soon."

"I feel it some already," Corinne said. "Don't you a little?"

"I feel it a little, all right."

Corinne sat on the bed and made the ice tinkle in the glass. When she smiled, her lips unsheathed saliva-bright teeth. Acel sat down beside her on the edge of the bed. "I've just been thinking that girls like you ought to go to heaven. This is the best time I've had in a long time. I was lying in a park not so long ago, and I saw a couple pettin', and I wondered then how long it would be before I had someone. It's mighty nice sittin' here and looking at you and knowing that you are mine."

He bent over her, pressing his mouth on her lips and holding her tighter. She stroked his back. . . .

Corinne came out of the bathroom and got a cigarette off the dresser. "I have an uncle who is a cashier in a restaurant over in Astoria, and he says this N.R.A. is going to put a lot of men to work in cafés. Maybe he could give you a job."

Acel got up off the bed. "You wouldn't want no bus boy for a sweetie, would you?"

"I had rather have you that than a sailor in Africa or some place."

"Don't you worry about me gettin' a job," Acel said. He poured gin into the two glasses. "I'm liable to have a real one pretty soon. You've heard of Red Gholson, haven't you? Well, there's a man who's promised to give me a job. I mean Red Gholson, too. I'll show you some of my clippings in a minute."

They drank the liquor.

Acel brought the newspaper clippings out of the big soiled envelope and spread them on the dresser. Some of them were yellow and broken. He pointed out his name and identified himself in the photographs of orchestras.

"I didn't know you could sing."

"Sure. 'Course I'm not any big shot, but I could do more in a band than double-tongue a trumpet. I can dance, too. I don't mean amateur stuff in that, either. If I ever get hold of a band, I've got some publicity ideas that will work. I'll have me a band some of these days."

"I hope you stay in New York."

"Don't you worry about that."

"What are you going to do tomorrow?"

"I don't know. I know this, though, I can get a lot drunker on you than I can on this stuff."

"I was thinking that you could come out to the house. I could tell my aunts that you drove me down from Connecticut, that I just waited and came with you. Don't you tell them, now, or say anything about being out of a job or working on a boat. I'll tell them you are a musician."

"Don't your aunts like old salts?"

"Sure enough now, don't you say anything, Ace. My aunts are funny."

"Here, honey, here's another drink."

"I don't want one this time."

"You going to be a sissy on me?"

"I don't want one this time."

Corinne showed Acel her memorandum book. In it were pasted a lot of poems, most of them by Dorothy Parker. There was a letter from a boy in school, and she showed this. It was illustrated with pen sketches that depicted grief and loneliness and love.

"This guy must be sweet on you."

"Don't you think these drawings are cute?"

"That's what I got against you women. Now this fellow here probably thinks you're in church tonight."

"He's not thinking about me. This letter is three months old. He's got a girl, you can bet."

Acel poured another drink. "How many sweethearts you had?"

"Not very many. I've just had two, really sweethearts."

"Just two, uh?"

"Just two really."

"I've had a bunch of sweethearts."

They lay on the bed. Corinne said her first sweetheart was the brother of her best girl friend. He worked in Wall Street and had a Cadillac. She never did get to drive the Cadillac, though. She had an abortion. He lost his job in the crash and was in California now. Once in a while she got a letter from him saying he was going to send for her.

"I guess you wish he would, don't you?" Acel said.

"Sometimes."

"I guess you're still pretty sweet on him?"

"I don't think about him much. My aunts throw it up to me, and sometimes I get tired of staying at home."

Acel cleared his throat. "How many affairs you had?"

Her head moved on the pillow toward him. "Not many."

"How many you had, like us here?"

"I don't make a habit of this."

"Nineteen? Twenty?"

"I am not as common as you think I am."

"A couple of hundred?"

Corinne got up. "You are getting smart now." She slid off the edge of the bed and stood above him. He stared at her sullenly. "You don't have any business talking to me that way," she said.

"You haven't answered me yet," he said.

Her navel showed through the damp, twisted pajamas. "I knew I should not have come up here with you. I wouldn't have come up here with you if I had known you were going to act this way. It isn't too late for me to go home."

"Forget it," Acel said. "I'm just poppin' off. It's none of my business. I know that. Forget it." He got up and reached out to touch her, but she drew back against the dresser.

"Hell, honey, you're not going to get sore about it, are you? What are you so mad about? I didn't mean anything. I spoke out of turn, all right, but golly, don't get mad about it. Jesus Christ. You're not going to get mad about it, are you?"

Corinne began straightening the damp pajama jacket.

"C'mon, honey, I didn't mean anything. No use of gettin' this mad over nothing. Why, honey, I'm not good enough for you to wipe your . . . your feet on. Don't be mad."

"You have no business talking to me that way."

"I know it, honey. You don't have to keep telling me. Here, honey, let me just hold your hand."

"I would not have come up here with you if I had known you were going to act this way."

"Aw, Jesus Christ. Let me kiss your hand, honey. . . . Just your hand. . . . That's a girl. . . . You're sweet. . . . I'm not going to be able to get along without you. . . . Let's take another drink, and then we got to get some sleep."

13
HANGOVER

CORINNE would not take a drink. She was going home now, and she did not want it on her breath.

They stopped at a café near the ferry station, but they only drank the coffee and left the sweet rolls untouched.

They sat forward on the ferryboat and watched the Manhattan shore line push toward them like a mammoth postcard. "You will be out all right tonight?" Corinne said. "You know how to get there now all right?"

Acel nodded.

They walked from the ferry station to the elevated railway and stood by the newsstand. "Maybe you would like a paper to read going home?" Acel suggested. "The *News?* . . . The *Mirror?*"

She shook her head.

"Don't you want to ride a taxi home?"

"No, the subway is just right up there. This is your L here."

"Which side of this L do I go up on to get to South Ferry? I'm always turned around in this damned town."

"This is the side."

"Well, I guess we might as well say good-bye?" Acel said.

"I will see you tonight?"

Acel nodded. "Be a good girl." He watched her cross the street and then turned and began the Elevated climb. His stomach burned.

* * *

The sun lay on South Street like a blistering plaster, glaring up from the sidewalk. The chowder smell from the curb lunch wagon nauseated Acel. A man in a sweat-discolored felt hat and with a finger missing on his left hand dragged ahead of him. Acel spurted by.

At the cigar stand in the lobby of the Seafarers' Home he bought a sack of Bull Durham. The tobacco smoke was like hot water on his lungs, and he dropped the cigarette.

Lungdren was not in the lobby. That guy may still be around here, Acel thought. He went up into the recreation hall, but Lungdren was not there, nor in the writing room, nor in the washrooms.

Acel came out of the Home and stood on the curb. A squat figure in a blue serge suit, smoking a pipe, came across the street toward him. It was Boats.

"You haven't seen Lungdren around, have you?" Acel said.

"Didn't you know about him?"

"What?"

"I thought you knew. He's dead. Two months."

"Lungdren is?"

"Didn't you know it?"

"I'll be goddamned."

"Let's go over to the Wobbly and get some coffee," Boats said.

"That's the damnedest thing I ever heard of. It makes me want to puke. That's the way it makes me feel."

The coffee burned in Acel's stomach like hot lead. He drew his forefinger across his forehead and flung the sweat on the floor. "How long you been ashore, Boats?"

"I been back two weeks. I'm shipping boatswain on the *Seagal* next month. It's going to be a long trip. How would you like to come along?"

"Naw, I don't know."

"We're going to Frisco, and I know I could get you signed on there."

"Naw, I think I'm going to hang around here. You know, I told Lundgren he ought to do something for that cold. I kept wondering why I never heard from him. Pneumonia, uh?"

"A man can't starve himself and expect to fight pneumonia."

"I guess so."

A man with a bowl of soup cupped in both hands worked cautiously past their table and lowered it carefully on the adjoining table.

"So you quit the *Picfair?*"

"Yeah."

"I don't blame you."

"Yeah. I'm planning on hanging around here in New York. I'm going to get a shore job. I got a girl I kind of like."

"You got a pretty nice front on you there. Where did you get that suit?"

"I got this, anyway. I got that much out of that boat anyway."

"So you got you a girl now?"

Acel nodded. "Pretty nice girl."

A counterman came and tacked up a placard on the wall above their heads: *Bread, beans & coffee, 10¢.*

"Where you stayin'?" Acel asked. "The Seafarers'?"

"No, I'm on their black list sure enough now. They won't hardly let me come in the lobby now. I'm staying in a two-bit place over on the Bowery. They're just stalls, but they'll give you a quarter for every bedbug you find."

"Chicago's a good place to get by in if you just got a few nickels. There's a place there they call the Legion Hotel. For two bits you get a flop and coffee and rolls for breakfast and soup in the afternoon."

"That's pretty good. Chicago's a pretty good town."

"I wish I had me a good job just for a couple of months," Acel said. "I don't mean this dollar-a-day business."

"You busted?"

"No, I got a few dollars. It won't last while you got a girl, though."

"Where does she live?"

"Over in Brooklyn about a million miles."

"We're having a little meeting tonight, some of the boys. We're going to get up petitions asking the Seafarers' to open up that fifth floor and make a dormitory of free beds out of it. We're going to ask them to start putting out a free meal every day, too."

"They won't give you nothing over there."

"How would you like to meet with us?"

"I'm going to see my girl tonight."

Acel found the house in Brooklyn at last. It was a three-story frame house with bay windows and a "Room for rent" sign. There was a sign, "Ice," over the basement entrance, and in the doorway stood a man in a black shirt smoking a cigar.

On the third story was Apartment 3-F. Acel knocked on the door, and then a tall woman in a black silk dress and lace collar stood there. Her face was shiny and porous.

"May I see Corinne?"

"She does not live here any more."

"You mean she does not stay here?"

"She is not here," the woman said.

Acel descended the stairway and passed the ice man. He went on down to the corner and looked at the display of bottles in the grocery-store window. The ginger ale was three for a quarter. In Jersey he and Corinne paid two bits for two bottles. Things were cheaper here in Brooklyn.

"Nice weather," the ice man said.

Acel nodded and went up the stairway again to Apartment 3-F.

Steps approached the door firmly, and then the door opened and the woman in the black dress stood there again.

"Would you tell me where Corinne moved?"

"I could not."

Another woman came and stood in the doorway. She was plump, and her hair was plastered down as if she had been to the beauty parlor.

"I was to see her tonight, and that's why," Acel said.

"She does not live here, and we do not know where she is," the plump woman said.

On the subway Acel thought he might just ride it the rest of the night. The papers said hundreds of fellows and girls rode the subways all night. The people in this car, though, didn't look like people who would ride the rest of the night. Those two fellows there with wrist watches, they're not all-night subway riders. And that girl there with the hatbox isn't. That old man there might. The girl with the hatbox got up and moved toward the center of the car. Under the diaphanous chiffon of her dress the curving outline of her tight undergarment moved on her thighs. Corinne's panties showed through her dress like that.

Acel got off at Fifth Avenue and walked up to Central Park. The band was playing in the Mall. He sat on a bench and watched skaters go by in churning streams.

A blonde, loose-breasted woman and a little boy sat on a bench next to Acel. The boy kept wandering off, and the woman would get up and call him until he returned. She looked like that blonde woman in the tabloids, the one they were trying upstate for poisoning her husband, Acel thought.

When the little boy unbuttoned his trousers, his mother laughed about it and looked at Acel and smiled. The child tottered over to Acel and stood before him with his hands held up and his elbows on his stomach.

"What have you got to say, big boy?" Acel said.

The child struck at Acel and then wobbled back to his mother.

14
ANN

WITH Corinne's letter, Acel waited in Battery Park for the fixed hour of their meeting. Three pleasure steamers lay alongside the landing, their decks aflame with holiday seekers. Out of the flashing bells of the musicians' instruments at the rails came spurring gusts in Harlem tempo. Water-soaked boys swam underneath the passenger-lined rails begging for pitched nickels. Excursion barkers moved in the dock crowds with the airs of circus ringmasters.

"Mr. Stecker, I believe," Corinne said.

Acel jumped up. "Hello there, Corinne." She was wearing the grey tunic coat, and her lips looked brighter with paint.

"I begin to think you weren't going to show up," Acel said. "I begin to get worried."

"I am not late, am I?"

"I guess not. It's okay."

They sat on the bench.

"Why didn't you wait for me the other night?" Acel said. "You could have waited on the corner or something."

"I did. I waited a long time. I just thought you were not coming. I thought I was stood up."

"I was a little late, but I got off at the wrong station and got all balled up, but you ought to have known I would have been there."

"I started to not even write you. I did not know how you felt about it."

The whistle on the stack of the largest steamer groaned in a little cloud of white steam, and the deckhands attacked the gangplank as if their jobs depended on doing it in two minutes. She parted from the dock sluggishly, like a gorged sea mammal, and then, her screw kicking up a taffy spray, slid releasedly toward the East River.

"Damit, honey, I wish you and me were on that boat. You sure can have a good time on a boat, can't you?"

"I hate to see boats go. They always make me blue."

"We'll take a trip some of these days. Up to Bear Mountain."

Corinne nodded.

Acel's finger went into his watch pocket. "While I think about it, you better take this money here."

Corinne pushed his hand back. "No, I don't want to do that. You need that yourself."

"Now don't start any of that stuff. It's bad enough the dab it is."

"No, there is not any use of that. I don't want to."

"Why isn't there some use? This is enough to get you by for a few days. A lot can happen in a few days. I'm going to look up Gholson. I'm going to tell him this time that my wife is here and I have to have something to do."

A flake of a man in a shriveled seersucker suit went by with a yellow roll of paper under his arm.

"Are you my girl, or are you?" Acel said.

"Of course I am, darling."

"That's all I want to know."

"I did not know for sure whether you even thought about me or not after we left. I did not know whether to write you or not."

"You know now, and I want you to take this money. You got to have a place to stay until I kind of get on my feet."

"I have a place to stay for a while. You do not have to worry about that."

"Where are you stayin'?"

"With Ann."

"Who is Ann?"

"She's a good friend of mine. You'd like her. I can stay with her."

"Where does she live?"

"On Fifty-first."

"What does she do?"

"It's a sort of a little tearoom. She sells liquor."

"A joint, uh?"

"You can call it that if you want to."

"That's what it is. I thought so. You're stayin' in a whore house, uh?"

Corinne got up. "You're going to be reasonable now or I'm not going to stand here and talk to you. Ann is as square as she can be. I told her about you, and she understands."

"I guess you told her I was a bum."

"I most certainly did not. I know you are going to be somebody some day. The difference is that you can sleep on park benches and get by now. Ann says that a down-and-out man begs and a woman sells."

"So that's it. I thought so. I figured that." Acel got up. "So that's what you're going to do?"

"Good-bye, Ace."

"Wait a minute. Sit back down here." Acel thumbed at the bench. Corinne returned and sat down.

"I can't pull money out of the air," Acel said. "I can't do that."

"I know it. But you don't have to say anything about Ann."

"So you're stayin' with a whore?"

Corinne got up again. "I am not going to stay here another minute."

"That's okay with me."

Corinne looked at Acel sharply, and he reached out and grasped her hand. "Now wait a minute, let's figure this out."

Corinne looked toward the boats.

"Take this money and stay some place just for a couple of days. I don't want you going around that place, Corinne. I'm not going to be long about gettin' a job, and then everything will be okay. You just wait and see if you don't believe it. There's enough for you to get by on for a few days. I'm tellin' you, Corinne, I'll have a job pretty soon. Let's figure this out now. Corinne, I'll swear."

15
FIFTY BUCKS

THE stirring leaves above Acel and Boats rattled like type-writers behind closed doors. Acel sat with his knees drawn under his chin, staring across the sloping grass of Central Park toward the shaft of Columbus Circle.

Boats spat the blade of grass off his tongue. "Now you take you going around and trying to get a hashing job. You're equipped to entertain people with music. There's a lot of music-hungry people in this world. They are denied music, and you are denied the chance to entertain them. Any clodhopper can beat you washing dishes, and if I was a boss I had rather have him. You should be doing the thing you can do the best, and the reason you are not is because under this system of government they call de-mocracy one man can pay a crooner one thousand dollars for one night and another man can't let his child give a penny to a grind organ."

"I got to get something to get by on awhile."

"If you went on the *Seagal* you could get some money ahead."

"I'd like to make a real trip like that, but I'd be just like I am now when I got back. I can't get a job in an orchestra on a freighter out in the middle of the ocean, and there is no use of trying to have a girl if you go to sea."

"I wish I could tell you what to do."

"Something is going to happen."

The approaching policeman was smacking the soles of park sleepers. Acel and Boats got up and moved toward Columbus Circle.

"What do you think about these girls that hustle for a living?" Acel said.

"I have as much respect for a woman who sells her body for pleasure as I do for these sweatshop slaves and these girls in these cheap department stores. Take all these women running back and forth from these offices. They are prostituting their minds and their hands to make some man richer. As long as a country is run to make men rich there will be harlots and robbers. I can't understand these men who claim to be Christians. Jesus Christ was a Socialist, and damn near every preacher crucifies him to this day. That's why I spit on the church."

Acel nodded. "I've thought that the difference between a bank president and a bank bandit is that the robbery of the banker is legal. The bandit has more guts. I think that's the reason bandits are made heroes by the public, because people sort of sense that there isn't much difference."

"You got it right there. When I see one of these rich women with a fistful of diamonds, I think that there goes a woman who represents a half-dozen bums, a bunch of whores, and a bunch of dead babies. I don't see how they can call a country like this civilized. What they mean is that they've civilized murder. Even a dog when he gets his guts filled will go off and let another dog have the carcass, but not man. He'll eat his fill and either put the carcass in cold storage or peddle it for thirty-three and a third per cent. Then they say there is a heaven for man and when a dog dies he's dead all over."

"I've always figured," Acel said, "I mean for a long time, that we don't know what it is all about. We're just a bunch of microbes living on a big body, the earth. Just a bunch of germs, and we know just about as much what it's all about as the germs do in our own bodies."

They stopped and looked at the display of silk socks in the Times Square shop window. They were fifteen cents a pair.

"I wouldn't mind having a job clerking in a store," Acel said.

"I despise these sentimentalists," Boats said. "Guys that drop a coin in a beggar's cup and consider it heaven insurance."

The sign in the stairway lobby amid a display of photographs of dancing girls read: *Are you lonely in the Big City? One hundred beautiful hostesses. Ten cents a dance. No extra charge.*

"I tried to get a job up there," Acel said. "They got a couple of bands."

The barker in front of the flaming canvas had long sideburns. "In the flesh, gentlemen, in the flesh. We do not appeal to the base in men. That is not our purpose with this exhibition. This is educational. But I'll tell you men that if you are red-blooded and virile, regular he-men, you will know that you are men when you see this. And just for today, gentlemen, in the flesh, mind you, fifteen cents. That's all. Fifteen cents. And you see everything, in the barc, naked flesh. . . ."

They walked on. "It's all in bottles," Acel said. "I've got hooked."

"Things like that are the eruptions of our moralists. What the moralists in this country need is a good physic. They are encouraging race suicide and perversion."

The young orator in front of the library flung out his hand. "Don't tell me I don't know what revolution is. My father died in Moscow. But how did the leaders of our Communist party go to Washington? How did they? In airplanes. How did me and my comrades go? In a Model T truck without brakes."

The Teutonic-headed man with his arms folded across his chest said: "Don't you think our leaders should go in style?"

"We should all go alike. We should all dress alike. Our Communist leaders dress like Jim Walker and have a different woman every night."

"Do you think our leaders should go like bums?" the Teuton said. "Do you think overalls should be the uniform of our party?"

"No, but they don't have to look like Lexington Avenue and ride in Packards."

Acel and Boats left the gathering around the young speaker and went over and leaned on the balustrade overlooking Fifth Avenue.

"I listened to a nigger over there one day," Acel said. "He said the black man would rule the world some day. He said everybody was black in the first place, but a bunch of humans have bleached out."

Boats laughed.

"I can't get interested in that sort of speaking, though," Acel said. "I mean that bunch over there. Some guy will say the world is round, and there'll be another dope who'll jump up and say it's a triangle and offer to go in the library and prove it. They argue over there like they were going to cut each other's throat."

"Some of them don't know what they're talking about, all right."

"This isn't gettin' me a job, standing here, spittin' on the sidewalk. Listen, Boats, I got to get some money."

Boats looked at Acel sharply.

"I'm going to tell you something, see? I've been thinking about it a whole lot. Now don't think I'm bullin'. I know a fellow here that's got plenty, and he's making plenty of money and I can see him. He's got a ring that's worth plenty. I can get it."

"What do you mean, stick him up?"

"Yeah."

"With your finger?"

"I can get a gun."

"You're talking like a crazy man now."

"I told you I was serious."

"You'd be about as good a hijacker as I am a horn blower. Don't think I'm getting righteous, but leave hijacking to the guys that know something about it. Why don't you take this girl and you two go get you a little dump some place and give yourself a chance? You could live on almost nothing."

"Not on nothing, though."

Boats spat over the balustrade. "I like to hit that bird going there."

"I'm either going to sleep in a jail or a house," Acel said. "I'll be damned if I sleep in any more stalls."

"Listen, why don't you do like I said? You get this girl and you two get you a little place somewhere. I'm shipping out in a couple of weeks, see? and I got fifty bucks I'm not going to need. Don't worry, I'll get it back from you."

"Where you got fifty bucks?"

"I worked all summer. Don't worry about that."

16

Mr. and Mrs. Stecker

Acel had lettered the slip above the brass mailbox himself: *Mr. and Mrs. Acel E. Stecker.* He looked at it now as he opened the empty box. Shifting the bundle and the small cardboard box back under his right arm, he went down the hallway and turned and started up the stairway.

The apartment of the Steckers overlooked the alley. There were two rooms, one which contained a cook range, a dining table, and a curtained kitchen table which concealed the bathtub; the other, a bed and a mirror. Clothing hung on the walls of the smaller room. In the larger, too, there was a small table on which some day they expected to place a radio. On it now lay the book by Bernard Shaw.

Acel unwrapped the bundle on the kitchen table. It was a bottle of gin. If she squawks about this, I'll tell her that she didn't say anything when I bought two bottles over in Jersey. It isn't going to hurt anything with Boats coming to eat with us tonight.

It was only a little after five o'clock, and Acel had an hour to wait for Corinne. She worked afternoons at the newspaper office, soliciting classified advertisements over the telephone. She got ten per cent commission.

Acel raised the window and looked down into the alley. A bunch of kids were playing with a rubber ball. A woman on the roof across the alley was taking clothes down from a line. A truck honked, and the children took their time getting out of its path.

Acel turned back and looked around the room. He could go out and get the steak, but Corinne had warned him about that. There was no icebox, and the thing to do was to wait until the last minute. He could peel the potatoes, though, and put them in cool water so they would stay crisp.

After he peeled the potatoes he went over and counted the packets of razor blades in the cardboard box. There were fourteen. That was what he had thought. That made twenty-two packs he had sold that day. One dollar and ten cents clear.

He looked out the window again. The kids were gone. The trouble about living in the back of a joint was that you couldn't see if anybody was coming. You didn't know they were here until the knob turned in the door. Seven flights of stairs was too much for a girl to have to climb. It made a man puff.

Corinne came in with the meat and lettuce and a jar of strawberry preserves. She showed Acel the runner in her stocking. "Can you beat that?" she said.

Acel scraped the grease out of the can into the potato pot. "I sold twenty-two packs today."

"That's good," Corinne said. "I did not do so bad today. I sold twelve dollars' worth of ads."

"What I got to do is get a side line," Acel said. "Abe was showing me some cards today I believe I can sell. And some booklets. French stuff."

"Women?"

"Yeah."

"You don't want to start around with that kind of thing now."

"What's the difference? It would just be a side line, and you make four times more off of them than you do razor blades."

"You don't have to sell those things."

"Why, did you ever see any?"

"Yes."

"Where did you ever see any?"

"I don't know, I forget. I don't know."

"At that damned Ann's, I'll bet." Acel dropped the potatoes in the boiling grease and jumped back with the splutter.

"I wish you didn't have to just sell around South Ferry," Corinne said. "Why do you have to just be around down there all the time?"

"I know a bunch of seamen, that's why."

"You could sell a lot more uptown. Why don't you stay around this part of town?"

"I couldn't sell snowballs in hell up around here."

"You and that Boats." Corinne went into the bedroom.

"Hey, Corinne, I got us a little bottle of gin."

Corinne came to the door. She was in a slip and was running her hands up through the gingham house frock. "What did you get that for?"

"I thought we'd have a few drinks tonight."

Corinne lifted the dress and began pulling it down about her head. "So you and Boats can get drunk?"

"There you go. Boats doesn't even drink. What do you think about that? Now that's something else you got to hand him. Don't think I haven't noticed you digging him. I don't suppose I should have gotten it."

Corinne came over and took the fork out of Acel's hand and stirred up the potatoes.

"It just cost fifty cents," Acel said.

"Oh, I don't care, honey. I just don't like to see you around down there so much. Boats is always . . . always . . ."

"Always what?"

"Always preaching. You are not going to get anywhere as long as you run around with him. You're not a sailor. What good is it doing you?"

"I'm not going to argue with you. What do you mean, not doing me any good? Because I'm not making fifty dollars a week?"

"No, that is not it. I mean what good is all this talking around about seamen going to do you?"

"You mean about the petitions? That's not talking, that's taking action. I've got two hundred names on my petition, and Kasha has almost that many. Boats has about four hundred, and there's some more out. That's not talking. They are going to do something about it down at the Seafarers' this time, I'll bet you. They can't look at a thousand names of seamen and then fail to do anything."

Acel washed the dishes and Boats dried them. Corinne, barelegged, mended the runner in the stocking. When the dishes were finished, the men seated themselves at the table, and Boats filled his pipe. Corinne went into the bedroom and put on her stockings.

"So you think we ought to present the petitions tomorrow?" Acel said.

Boats nodded. "Yes, because I can't wait much longer now, leaving Monday. We got enough names. I think they'll come across."

"You want Kasha to go in with us to see the Judge?"

"Yeah. Three is just enough."

Corinne came out. "What are you going to do tomorrow?"

"I told you, honey," Acel said.

"We are going to show Judge Ross the petitions," Boats said.

"You want to talk to him straight and plain," Acel said. "Just put them on his desk and say, 'Look here.' "

"I will tell him that these petitions represent the sentiment of eight hundred seamen against the manner in which the Home is being operated. I will tell him that these seamen feel that if the Home continues to raise money and get endowments on the grounds that it is providing homeless seamen with food and shelter, that it will have to start seeing to it that jobless seamen do get some benefit or we will hold demonstrations all over New York."

"They got it coming to them."

"I'll tell him that if the salaries of executives must be cut in order to help these seamen, then the salaries must come down. I'm going to put in, too, about the hiring around there of men who know nothing about the sea."

"They got it coming to them, all right."

"I want you and Kasha to be there just to sort of lend moral support. If they get on a high horse, we'll go out in the park and make some talks and get up a crowd. I think the Judge will listen to us, though. If we got any hotheads started down there, it would be just too bad. We don't want any trouble. Then they would have an excuse to yell Bolsheviks and Reds and call the city cops. Caution everybody to keep cool, see?"

After Boats left, Acel cleaned the saucer they had used for an ashtray at the sink and dried it. He looked at the picture of the radio crooner's wife in the tabloid who was suing for divorce, and then read the story. After that he turned off the light and went into the bedroom.

Corinne had on the blue pajamas tonight. She lay on her side and did not look up. Acel undressed, turned out the light, and then went over to the window on the fire escape and lifted the shade. It ran to the top.

"I'll be damned if I get that down now," he said.

Acel lay on the bed and listened to the clock ticking in the next room. An elevated train's roar drowned the ticking, and after it was gone Acel tried to pick up the ticking sound again, but a fog horn sounded on the river. He turned over again cautiously.

Corinne reached out and placed her hand on his breast. "What are you thinking about?"

"Aren't you asleep? Aw, I don't know. I was thinking about tomorrow."

Corinne pressed closer, and Acel's arms went around her, and his lips found her mouth. Her fingernails cut into his flesh.

17
MUTINY

MACK WINTERS, chief of police in the Seafarers' Home, was
a tall man with a crop of hair like steel wool. He sat now
at his desk looking up at the three men, Boats, Acel, and
Kasha.

"Judge Ross has refused to see us," Boats said. "I have
come to you to tell you that we represent more than four
hundred seamen and feel entitled to an audience." He
placed the soiled petitions on the desk. "There are nearly
eight hundred signatures on these petitions. I have the
consent of these men and am urged by them to present
them formally to Judge Ross. I believe the claims we have
are just."

Winters stood up and took off his glasses. There were
colorless dents on the bridge of his nose. "What claims do
you have?"

"You may read the petition there. The details I will give
the Judge. What I am asking you to do is tell the Judge
we want to see him."

Winters looked at Acel. "Who are you? What are you
doing here?"

"I'm a member of the committee."

"You're a Communist, aren't you?"

"He's an American seaman," Boats said.

Kasha blew his nose.

Winters looked at Boats. "How would you like to do six months in jail?"

"You mean you think you can send me to jail? What's holding you? I'm no kid, Winters, don't pull that stuff on me. Are you going to arrange for us to give these petitions to the Judge or not?"

"I am going to do this for you. We have told you to stay out of this place. It is not a place for Reds or Anarchists or Fascists or anything else but Americans. Now if you ever come in this place again I am going to file charges against you myself."

"That's the way it is?" Boats said.

"I mean it, too." Winters lifted his finger. "And that goes for both of you, too. We don't want your kind around here."

The three men left the Home and crossed the street into the park. Men followed them, surrounded them when they stopped. The circle grew.

Boats got up on a bench and held up his hand, palm outward, and then with his left hand pointed across the street. "They've told us to kiss their ass!"

"Give 'em hell, Boats," a seaman in an oiler's cap shouted.

Acel and Kasha steadied the bench. Boats slapped his chest. "Are we American seamen going to stand here and allow ourselves to be prostituted by a politician they call a judge who sits up there in a three-room office and gets seven thousand dollars a year? Are we going to allow a man who used to walk a beat around and gets three thousand dollars a year now to see to it that we can't see this politician and tell him we need shelter and we need food?"

"Tell it to 'em!"

"Pour it on 'em!"

"Give 'em hell!"

Boats waved the petitions above his head. "They've told the eight hundred men whose names are on these sheets to go to hell. That's what it amounts to. What we ask is just and right. They raise money in our names, and why aren't we entitled to some of it when we need it? Are we seamen or are we men who paint our faces? How many of you men will go into that place with me?"

Acel got up on the bench. Kasha supported him. "I'll follow him," Acel shouted. "I'll follow him!"

Boats got down and, with Acel and Kasha at his sides and a crowd of fifty men following like a wedge, moved across the street.

The young policeman at the door turned and ran up the steps. The wedge entered.

Winters stood in the doorway of his office at the top of the broad stairway.

"Tell the Judge to come down and listen to us or we're going right on up to his offices," Boats said.

"Judge Ross is not in the building," Winters said.

"You're a damned liar," Boats said. "His Pierce is around the corner there. Get him down here or we're going up."

Winters withdrew into his office and closed the door.

The wedge surged into the already crowded lobby.

Boats clutched Acel's arm. "You tell this crowd here in the lobby what it is all about. Kasha and me and some of the rest will go on up to the Judge."

Acel climbed up on the water fountain. "Judge Ross won't look at the petitions eight hundred seamen have signed," he shouted. "Jobless seamen should have free beds and food. Politicians have no business in a place like this. . . ."

The loud speaker on the shelf high on the column in the center of the lobby began to roar: *All out of the building. Everybody out of the building. City Police are coming. . . . All out of the building. . . .*"

Acel pushed through the lobby crowds to the column. The seaman in the oiler's cap lifted him up, and he grasped the loud speaker and began wrenching at it. A glass, hurled from the lunch counter to the left of the lobby, shattered on the column. The seaman let Acel down. Acel's face was cut and bleeding. . . .

Sirens screamed outside . . . policemen came like boats

on waves of seamen, their clubs rising and falling like paddles. Pistol shots sounded above like the muffled collapse of a tin roof. *Everybody out of the building. . . . Everybody out . . .*

It was a whirlpool of clubs and fists and escaping bodies. It became a torrent, and the lobby throng poured out of the building into the street. . . .

The crowd was like a piano on Acel's back, and he strained to keep his feet, reach the park. The seaman with the wiper's cap clutched his arm and shook him. "You better wipe your face and get the hell out of here while the gettin' is good. Real hell has happened over there. Somebody is hurt."

Policemen were coming across the street into the park now. Acel ran.

18

CRIMINAL ASSAULT

ACEL sat there on the chair looking at the jersey silk undergarment on the line above the stove. Corinne called them panties. When they were washed they were not much bigger than your hand. He listened for Corinne's steps in the hallway. She had gone out for gauze and iodine and newspapers.

The food on the table had not been touched. There was Swiss cheese and pickles and crackers. Acel looked at the coffee pot on the stove. I bought that the second day, he thought. It was twenty-five cents. It seemed like a long time ago, but it just seemed that way.

He had held the one-legged man up under the shower in that Columbus flop house. That was a long time ago. The man had a stomach that bobbed like jelly. The flophouse men had made them dip their feet in a bucket of something before they let them under the showers. It was to prevent toe itch. He had wanted to ask the one-legged man if he had got the leg cut off under a train. It's funny how I sit here and think of things like that.

He had argued with the war veteran in Philly. The veteran was a lunger, and when they cut his pension he had to leave Arizona. He put his wife and kid on the bus and started highwaying it out of Phoenix. He stood there all day, and nobody stopped, so he got a freight train. He was dumb, though. He said the bonus marchers made the President sore, and that was why the pensions were cut. I called him on that. I shouldn't have argued with a lunger, though.

Corinne came in. She placed the newspaper on the table and began unwrapping the gauze.

"Paper say anything?" Acel said.

"It is in there, all right."

"What does it say?"

"He's dead, all right."

"Boats is?"

"Yes. Now hold your head up and I'll paint this."

After Corinne painted Acel's cuts with iodine, she lit the gas and put the coffee pot over the blaze. She stood there and watched the pot.

"A man has to die sometime," Acel said. "It won't make any difference a thousand years from now. Hand me the paper."

Footsteps sounded in the hallway, and Corinne looked toward the door. The steps faded, and a door opened and closed. The newspaper crackled as Acel turned the page.

Corinne poured the coffee into cups. She sat down and waited until Acel dropped the paper on the floor. He got up and dragged his chair to the table. When he sat down he winced and touched his shoulder. "I guess I must have got a lick or something."

"I guess you noticed it in the paper, Ace. I am sort of worried about it."

"I guess they'll get some sort of case against me."

"What is criminal assault, Ace?"

"It's when you hit somebody."

"Does anyone know down there where you live? Did you ever tell anybody down there where you lived?"

"Don't start bawlin' now, Corinne. It's bad enough as it is. They can find out easy enough. I don't care."

"I was just thinking that if they don't know where to look for you, why, you can just not go back down there any more and maybe they'll forget about it."

Acel lifted the cup, but set it back down. "I've been sort of thinking I might just get out of town."

"If you just don't go back down there or anything they won't know where you are."

"They can find out easy enough. They had to call the city police in. That was dirty. That was dirty." Acel turned and looked at the panties on the line.

"You better drink your coffee while it is hot."

"I was thinking about Boats."

"Does he . . . who are his people?"

Acel shook his head.

"Drink your coffee, Ace."

Acel turned and lifted the coffee and gulped. He placed it back down and looked at Corinne. "I've done you a helluva lot of good. If I go down South maybe I can find something to do. I'll send for you."

Corinne nodded.

"It's not that I'm afraid of jail or anything. I'd just as soon be in jail as any place. The only thing, I may get a job down South and then I can send for you."

Corinne nodded.

Acel got up and went over and looked out the window on the darkened alley. In the window across the way a man stood beside a bed in his underwear. Acel turned back. "I ought to go down there where he is or something. It didn't even say where they got him. I never thought they'd kill anybody. They shouldn't have done that. That's a lie. He didn't have no gun. I know he didn't have no gun. Why didn't they fight with their fists? That's all he had. It doesn't even say where they got him now, does it? I guess it's the City Morgue. I ought to go down there."

"I'll go," Corinne said. "I'll see to it. I'll go. I'll see to it."

19
ON THE ROAD

THE soft glow of a spent sun toned the harshness of the slag-crusted railroad yard. Acel, concealed behind the string of sided cars, watched the corralled company of hoboes move up the yards. The two detectives herding them had on dark suits and light, wide-brimmed hats.

A youth in a sweat shirt dropped down from the bumpers of the car ahead and paused at sight of Acel. Then he approached. "You got out of sight, too?" he said.

Acel nodded. "We'll get by if we just keep low. Those bulls are taking them out on that side of the yards."

The corralled hoboes and the detectives passed out of sight.

"I don't want to miss this *manifest*," Sweat Shirt said. "A man could be in Atlanta tomorrow. I'd like to be in Atlanta this time tomorrow night."

"Those bulls are going to have their hands full holding that bunch. We'll work down toward the end of the yards in a minute."

"I'm just hoping none of those bulls decided to ride it out," Sweat Shirt said.

Up in the yards by the roundhouse a locomotive whistled . . . *twice!*

Acel and Sweat Shirt started up the string of cars, their feet crunching in the gravel, and pretty soon broke into a half-run.

The locomotive of the long freight puffed and labored as if held in a giant's leash. Acel and Sweat Shirt lay on their stomachs at the bottom of the high embankment outside the yards. The locomotive went by. On the rungs of the first oil car rode a dark-suited figure with a club in his hand.

Acel nudged Sweat Shirt. "Wait until ten or twelve cars get by."

Sweat Shirt nodded.

The cars lumbered by ... three ... four ... *faster*. Seven ... eight ... *faster*. The man with the club disappeared between the cars!

Acel went up the grassy incline on all fours. He crossed the track, ran alongside the rocking box car, clutched at the rung, and swung up and in between the cars on the bumpers. The wheels below began clicking in heightened speed. He clung stiffly, throwing his head from side to side expectantly.

"Getoffathere, goddam ..."

The voice of the detective standing on the right-of-way was like an explosion smothered in the grinding of the trucks. Hurled rocks spattered on the car's sides. Acel went up the end of the car to the top. The train's surface was clear. This car was a refrigerator, but the reefer was sealed, and Acel started back on the train in a crouching, hand-extended run. He leaped to the next, and this reefer was unsealed. He squeezed backwards into the trapdoor opening, clung for a moment, like a jack-in-the-box, and then dropped into the hole.

The hole was dark. An acrid fume choked his nostrils, and he turned and tried to peer through the wire mesh: *onions*. The floor was tin and dented like a big scrub board. After a while Acel lowered himself to the floor. The car began to bounce with a staccato roll, and he gripped the sides to ease the punishment. Pretty soon the roll lessened, and he stretched out with guarded slowness, pillowing his head on his arm. ...

The thing to do is not to think about her. When I get a job and can do something about it, then that will be the time to think about her. It doesn't do any good just to think. The thing to do is just put her out of my mind. . . .

I'm gettin' thirsty. I've never seen it fail. Every time I get a hot shot I start gettin' thirsty. Before I get out of the yards I want a drink. . . .

No, the thing to do is just not think about her. . . .

The car began to bounce violently again, and Acel sat up, lifting himself on his hands until the bumping lessened, and then he lay down again. . . .

If I had a drink now, this wouldn't be bad at all. I'm going to hold this train down until she stops. A hobo in a refrigerator hole and his throat feeling gluey! It would make a short story, one of those short short stories they print in *Liberty*. Writers got one hundred dollars for those stories.

There wasn't nothing, though, to just a hobo riding in a reefer. Something had to happen. It would be something if I got off at the division to get a drink and a bull nabbed me? And I got thirty days? When the train stopped, the hobo in the story would crawl out and make a run for the hydrant in front of the shanty. The bull would jump out and grab him and say: "You got your guts, you son of a bitch."

You couldn't put "son of a bitch" in a magazine, though. "You got your guts, you punk. You're going to take a little ride."

Nothing to that, though, just a hobo gettin' run in for riding a freight train and caught because he got off the train to get a drink. Those stories had to have surprises at the end.

The jail where they take this guy would look like that one in Fort Worth. It would stink like that one. The sergeant would write down the guy's name and then the charge: *trespassing on r.r. prop.*

The cell would be like that one in Portsmouth, just a plank with bedbugs in the cracks. As soon as the hobo got in the cell he would start yelling: "Don't a man get a drink around here? I want a drink of water." He'd claw at his throat and make strangling sounds and yell: "Water! Water!"

There would be a fellow in the next cell. He would say: "What's the matter, Mac?"

"I haven't had a drink all day. I want a drink. Bring me some water."

"What are you in for, Mac?"

"Train riding. Water! *Water!*"

The guy in the next cell would laugh. "You'll get it, all right, Mac. Don't worry. That's what you get in this man's town for riding freights. *Three days on water.*"

With a hundred dollars I could send for Corinne easy enough. She could come all way to New Orleans on that. She could do it on fifty dollars. Then I'd have fifty to get things ready. But there's no use of me thinking about it until I can do something about it. . . .

The sun pierced the hole of the still car like a knife blade. A green fly buzzed in attacking gyrations. Somewhere a power pump throbbed. Acel got up, rubbed his stiffened arm, and then climbed up the hole.

It was a jerkwater town. The highway ran alongside the track, a bright strip of pavement flanked by dust-filmed houses. Acel descended the rungs stiffly, and when he dropped to the gravel his numb feet ached with the jar.

The depot was a frame, scabby-green structure. Inside, it smelled of stale smoke and sawdust boxes. A telegraphic instrument clattered behind the closed ticket window. There was a padlock on the washroom.

Acel came out. His skin under the beard felt hot and sore. He moved across the tracks toward the filling station on the corner. There was a sign: *Hitch hikers keep hiking.* A man in overalls and with a forehead and long nose like a wire-haired terrier stood in the station door and watched Acel wash at the hose. The water slid off Acel's face like thin oil.

Acel combed his hair. "I went to sleep in a car set off here last night," he said. "I thought I'd be in Atlanta by now."

"There won't be any more freights through here until tonight," the man said.

"I thought I might blind a passenger. I guess a man can do it all right around here."

"I saw them pick one up with a shovel that tried it over there one day. The railroad had to bury him."

Acel recrossed the tracks and sat down on the low-railed lawn to the left of the depot. Below the filling station where he had washed was a two-story white house with a low white picket fence. A new Chevrolet was parked in front. Two men in shirt sleeves rocked in chairs on the porch. One of them was smoking a pipe.

Acel pinched off the burning end of the cigarette and, breaking the paper, poured the tobacco in the sack. For a little while longer he looked at the men on the porch and then, suddenly, got up and moved across the tracks toward them.

The men stopped rocking as Acel came through the gate and went up to them. "Could I do something around here for something to eat?" Acel said.

The fat one said, "You hungry, boy?"

"Yessir, I'd like to work for something to eat."

"Where you from, boy?"

"New York."

"You're a long ways from home, aren't you?"

"Yessir."

"You shouldn't have left home. I'll bet your folks would send for you if they knew you were out like this. Why don't you get them to send for you?"

"I don't have folks."

"You look like a boy that would work to me. You got a good face on you."

"I'll work, all right."

"I'm just boarding here myself, this fellow here and me, but the woman that runs this house is a good lady, and she will give you something to eat. I'll go in and tell her." The fat man got up and went into the house.

The other man was lean and wore suspenders. He did not look at Acel, but gazed across the tracks toward the depot.

The fat man came back. "She's fixing you up something." He lowered himself back into the rocker and went backward and forward for a few moments. "I'm a traveling man myself, but I don't pick up men on the highway. I'd like to, but it's too dangerous. There's too many men going around the country hungry, and you just can't take chances."

Acel nodded.

"I'd like to pick fellows up, but I just can't afford to take the chance. There was a man killed picking a fellow up here not so long ago. Killed him and took his car after he had picked him up. When was that, Bob? . . . Was it that long ago? . . . Six years. I didn't know it was that long."

The woman came out with the food wrapped in bread paper. She had on a checkered apron. Acel went up the steps, and she handed the food to him. "I'll be glad to do any work around here, lady."

"That is all right."

"I sure do thank you." Acel backed down the steps and then looked at the fat man. "Many thanks to you all."

"Wait a minute, boy." The fat man stood up and put his hand into his pocket. "You got a good face on you, boy. You look like a good boy to me. Here, here, I'm going to give you a dime. You can buy yourself some tobacco or something."

Acel caught the flipped coin. "Thanks. Many thanks, sir."

Acel went down to the red, peeling water tank and sat

down on the Bermuda grass. He unwrapped the bread paper: cold bacon, a biscuit with red jelly; dry, crumbly cake and two slices of light bread. After he ate he went over and began examining the writing on the legs of the water tank. There were some obscene drawings and rhymes.

The old man came up and lowered his pasteboard suitcase to the ground. His faded eyes looked out of cavelike sockets.

"Hello, Dad," Acel said.

"Hello." The old man began taking off his coat.

Acel left the water tank and approached the other. "How's the road treatin' you? Pretty good?"

"I ain't complainin'. Pretty good. Yessir, pretty good. I'm four days out of Daytona Beach. That's pretty good."

"You bet that's good. That's a lot better than I've been doing."

"It's pretty good for an old man."

"How old are you, Dad, anyway?"

"Seventy-four. Seventy-five this coming November."

"You sure don't look that old."

The old man pulled the suitcase toward him. "I got something in this bag here." He began undoing the rope around it. "I got something here."

It was a drawing of an airplane. Dad said it was a model of a humming-bird airplane and he was the inventor. He had showed it in Lindbergh's office in New York, he said, and now all he needed was twenty-five dollars to have a model made.

"Don't you have a family?" Acel said.

"Me? Yeah, I got a family." Dad returned the drawing to the suitcase and began fixing the rope around it. "Yeah, I got a family. Haven't seen none of them in twelve years, though. I've had family troubles, if you know what I mean."

"You had family troubles, uh?"

"Yeah, but I don't like to talk about it."

They watched the truck climb up to the crossing down the tracks, stop, go into low gear, and then labor over.

Dad said that before he started inventing and running around he had been a Baptist preacher.

"I've been thinking that if the preachers quit yelping about hell and prohibition and dancing," Acel said, "and took an interest in things that mattered, they would come a lot nearer emulating Jesus Christ. Why don't they drive out a few money lenders? They holler, 'Give to the poor,' but they don't realize that there is no need for the poor at all."

"I haven't preached in twelve years."

"I was in a jungle up the road night before last, and a bunch of us got to talking, and I told that bunch that we were just like a bunch of immigrants running around the country trying to find a place to dig in. In the old days they called us hordes and barbarians, but the men in those days had swords, and if the people who had plenty didn't share it, they took it. I told that bunch that every one of us should have a home and a wife and plenty to eat in a country like this, because there is plenty, and the trouble was that some men have more than they should. I asked if anyone there was a Socialist. One guy said something: 'I'm for better living,' he says. Godamighty. No wonder we're just scum. I'll bet you are a Socialist, aren't you, Dad?"

Dad nodded. "That's for young fellows, though. What I got to do is invent me some little something I can sell. There's a lot of money down in Florida, and I'm going back there this fall. I'm not going to sell pencils or anything like that, though. What I got to do is invent me some little something I can make myself."

A freight truck rumbled on the station platform, and Acel watched the station agent trundle it into place.

"So you've had family troubles, Dad?"

"Yeah, but I don't like to talk about them."

"I guess you busted up with your wife?"

"Yeah. But I don't like to talk about them. You know what I mean by family troubles. I don't like to talk about people that are dead. You know what I mean, though. She

liked men too much. That woman just liked it too much.
I saw it plain after it was pointed out to me that the kids
were his."

"You mean your kids weren't yours?"

"The oldest was mine. I never did tell nobody but him.
I saw it plain after it was pointed out to me."

"Did you know the man?"

"I reckon I did. He used to lead singing at my meetings.
But I don't like to talk about family troubles."

20

Chain-gang Country

THE lights of a restaurant's front lay on the sidewalk ahead like a bright tear in the black mantle of the street. It was after midnight. Somewhere a trolley car screeched at a turn and then rumbled on to fade into a singing murmur.

Pushing himself erect from the lamppost, the youth in the slip-over sweat shirt and suspenders stopped Acel: "You got a match?" His breath stank of alcohol.

Acel handed him the pack. "You know where the Muny is around here?"

The cigarette clung to the moist lips of the other and bobbed as he spoke. "You want to go with me?"

"Go to hell."

Acel went on and around the corner stopped a Negro. "You know where the Muny is around here?"

"The what?"

"The place where a man can get a free flop."

"Oh, now I knows what you mean. Sometimes I sees a bunch hanging around the city auditorium. Yeah, that's the place you wants. Now I knows what you mean. You go right down this street foah blocks and then foah thataway. Now I knows what you mean."

The free shelter slept. Acel rattled on the door and shook the knob, but there was no answer.

The trays of fruit in front of the stand at the corner

gleamed like metal under the street lamp. There was a policeman at the end in a white-billed cap and Sam Browne belt and a stand attendant in a soiled white apron. The policeman looked at Acel over the edge of a half-eaten slice of watermelon.

"Could you tell me, officer, where a man could get a bed this time of night who hasn't any money?"

The policeman took another bite of the melon and spat the seeds out with a quick twist of his head. "You're out of luck."

"I was just down to the municipal place, and they were closed up. I guess all the places are closed up now?"

The officer spat out another mouthful of seeds. "Yeah, they're closed."

"I guess it would be a good idea for me to go down to the police station and not hang around on the streets?"

"If you want to get locked up and spend the night with a bunch of drunks, you can."

"I wouldn't like that. Naw, I guess I can just sleep on a park bench somewhere."

"You don't sleep in parks in this town unless you want to be vagged."

"This is kind of a tough town."

"Tough." The officer tossed the rind into the gutter and looked back at Acel. "That's the trouble with this country, birds like you running around."

The head of the standkeeper began to go up and down.

"Where you from?"

"Memphis."

"I thought so. What did you leave there for?"

"I got a pretty good job prospect down in Jacksonville, and I didn't have any other way of getting there except beating my way. I got a pretty good chance to get a job, and I wanted to get there."

"You oughta stayed where you come from. That's the trouble with this country now, you bums running around and living off people."

The standkeeper's head bobbed.

"I'm paying taxes every year just to feed birds like you. That place right down there costs us a hundred thousand dollars a year just to keep birds that are here today and gone tomorrow. Have you been to the Salvation Army? . . . I don't know whether you can get in there or not. Don't think you can this time of night. You can go try it, though. You birds don't have any business leaving where you come from. Go on down there and try to get in there."

Acel followed the policeman's directions. Learned man, he thought. Paying taxes to keep bums up. Who is paying his hundred bucks a month? And that old belch standing there with head going up and down and feeding him watermelon. The bastards.

This is fun, runnin' around looking for a place to flop. I don't want to work. Me, want to work? It's too much fun running around from town to town and seeing the country from nice freight trains. It's the bums' fault. A bum shouldn't be running around the country without money. He should make it a point to have two or three hundred dollars when he gets in a town. He should attend to things like that. The big bastard. And that old belch standing there with his head going up and down . . .

The second shelter was open.

The farmer-looking transient with the whittled cane and slow, painful gait said he was walking in the direction of the railroad yards himself and would show Acel the way. Acel did not mind the slow gait of the other. It was Sunday morning, and the streets were almost deserted. The sunshine was cool.

"That wasn't a bad breakfast we had this morning in that place," Acel said. "That's a new one on me. Fried bread with bacon in it."

"We got it on the farm," Whittled Cane said. "I just got out. A year and a day I did."

"Just got off a prison farm, uh?"

"Year and a day." Whittled Cane said he was sent up for firing some woods down in the southern part of the state, but he didn't no more do it than Acel did. He said he was ruptured and didn't do a lick of work all the time he was there. He whittled canes and sold them to prison visitors.

"Prisons are the cancers of the capitalistic system," Acel said. "And bums are its boils."

"I didn't do a lick of work while I was there."

They waited until the trolley car passed and then crossed the empty street.

"America is the richest country in the world and at the same time the most criminal. They can spend forty billion dollars for policemen and jails and put an electric chair in every town, and they won't stop it that way. They are going to have to open their eyes to more than that to stop it."

"You talk kind of like a feller I knew down there on the farm. He was one of them radicals, one of them Communists, like Jews and niggers. 'Course I don't mean to say you're like him."

"What was he in for?"

"Freight-train ridin'."

"You mean they got them on that farm for that?"

"They got a hundred out there for that."

"Hell, I didn't know that. I didn't know they were picking them up for that."

"Don't think they're not. There was a hundred of them in there."

Whittled Cane stopped and pushed the bright, coin-sized piece of metal with his stick. It was tin. "I'm headed for home myself," he said. "I haven't seen my old woman now for more than a year. The kids come down once, but the old woman stayed home."

"I guess you can stand to see her, all right, after a year in that place."

"The old woman's got pellagra pretty bad. She ain't much use to me that way any more. I was thinking about stopping at one of these hotels and seeing me a woman before I went on home."

"I got a wife back in New York," Acel said.

"The old woman's got pellagra pretty bad."

"So they had them in there for train riding?"

"Yeah."

"Might be a good idea if I highwayed it out of here like you are. Out of this state, by god. I sure didn't know that."

"Yeah, you make me think of that feller that was down there on the farm with us. There was one thing about that feller, he didn't take nothing off the guards. I'll bet they whipped his behind a thousand times. He was too thick with the niggers, though. He treated them like they was white."

21
BIG BOY

RAIN cracked against the sided box car at the edge of the yards in wind-driven sheets. Acel, in the warm and dry car, rewrapped the sack of tobacco and matches in the waxed bread paper and put it back in the bosom of his shirt. He felt over his watch pocket. Yes, the twenty-five cents was still there.

The car shivered in a fresh gust. Two weeks now he had been out of New York, and not a single time had he been caught in the train. That was pretty good. The other time it rained he was in that little town in North Carolina. He had been run out of the depot, but he had found a window open in that church. The church smelled of fresh paint, and he had slept on a bench with hymnals for a pillow.

A face peered in the box-car door. It was a square, Scandinavian face with a flattened, scarred forehead.

"Come on in, Big Boy," Acel said. "It's pretty dry in here."

The man climbed in. He was big, with bulky shoulders and thick hands. He took off his soggy cap and shook it. "Kind of wet outside."

"It's pretty wet, all right," Acel said.

Big Boy took off his coat and shook it and then hung it on a nail on the door. He came over then and sat down on the other side of the car facing Acel.

"Which way you headed?" Acel said.

"North."

"I'm headed west. New Orleans."

"I don't see what anybody wants to go there for. Ain't nothing in that town."

"It's pretty cheap there."

The door of the car rattled with the wind. Rain sprayed through it, and the two men moved deeper into the car.

"I ain't exactly decided where I will go," Big Boy said. "It don't make no difference to me much."

"One place is about as good as another when you're on the bum, I guess."

Big Boy crossed his legs. "I'm over the hill myself. You know what I mean, I guess?"

"Army?"

"Naw, the bug house. They say I'm crazy. I got more sense, though, than some of those fellows working that hospital, though. One of 'em asked me to shine his shoes, and I told him to go to hell and walked out of the place and went over the hill."

"How do they feed in those places?"

"Aw, pretty good."

"How do you get along with people in those places?"

"Aw, those fellows that run it are no good. They operated on me while I was in there. See, right here? I got a plate right here in my head. See, right there, see?"

"Uh."

"I had another plate in there, but it was pressing on my head. I got hit there in a fight when I was in the navy. A guy hit me with a marlin spike."

"You got a lick there, all right."

Rain sprayed into the car again, and Big Boy got up and slid the door almost shut. He felt of his coat and then came back. "Lots of robbing going on over this country now," he said.

"Bums are not doing much of it," Acel said. "Take these

box-car robberies. It's towners that are doing it. A bum doesn't have any way of carting the stuff off. Aw, they might get a couple of oranges once in a while, but it's the towners that are doing it, no matter if these bulls do lay it onto them."

They can rob 'em all as far as I'm concerned."

"I'm not going to run and tell anybody if I see it happening. I was reading the other day about a poor bastard who got five years for robbin' a pay telephone of eighty-five cents, and right beside him was a picture of a banker that got one year after the bank he was president of went busted. Things like that is what burns me up."

"Me, too."

"We're going to have revolution," Acel said. "People are not going to stand for stuff like that always. I'll be glad when it comes. The first thing the revolutionists will have to do away with the tin soldiers and flat-feet."

Big Boy's hand came out of his blouse with a flour sack in it. He put his hand into the bag and looked at Acel with an odd quirk on his lips.

"What you got? Somethin' to eat?"

Big Boy nipped the roll at Acel's feet. The money looked like a green bullfrog lying there.

"That looks like whether I'm crazy or not," Big Boy said.

"Jesus Christ," Acel said. "Is that the real stuff?"

"That don't look like I'm crazy, does it?"

"I wouldn't mind having a sack like that myself."

Big Boy bent forward and picked up the roll and began to bounce it on his flattened palm. "I knew your eyes would pop out," he said.

"You ought to be pretty careful showing that around."

"If a man thinks he can get it, he's welcome to try. I'm not half as buggy as some people think. This don't look like I'm crazy, does it?"

"Naw, that looks pretty good."

"What do you call yourself, buddy?" Big Boy said.

"Ace."

"How would you like to go get us a little something to eat? Some pork and beans or something?"

"I wouldn't mind it."

"I mean as soon as it quits rainin' some."

"It's okay with me."

Big Boy unfastened the roll and tossed a bill at Acel's feet. It was ten dollars. "I'm hungry as a bitch wolf myself," he said. "I could eat the hindin off a skunk."

Acel picked up the bill. "What kind of grub do you want?"

"Don't make no difference to me just so it is grub. If you see any of them there little chocolate cakes, get some of them. It don't make no difference to me. And you can put the rest of that in your sock."

"This money is okay, all right, I guess?"

"You're not afraid of it, are you?"

"I don't care if it is hot. I just don't want to fool with it if it's phony."

"If you're afraid, it's okay with me."

"I'm not afraid. It looks good to me. I'm going to change clothes, and you watch this bag while I'm gone. I'm going to put on a pretty good front so they won't look at me too much when I bust this ten."

"Now you're talking. That's the trouble with me, I can't look like anything in nothing."

Big Boy watched Acel dress. "You heard anything about them going to stop this train riding?"

"You hear that all the time. Everywhere a man goes, somebody is going to tell him he can't get out on a train. But I been gettin' out pretty good everywhere. I come all the way from New York on trains except one jump. It's tough highwaying down here. The folks down here are afraid of their shadows."

"It was in the papers that they're going to put marines on the trains and shoot bums off."

"They've been riding trains in this country ever since there's been trains, and they always will."

"That's the way I look at it."

22

BILL

THE freight train crawled guardedly across the high trestle, its trucks and beams grinding and swishing sluggishly. In the wide doorway lolled silent riders, silhouetted against the Gulf and a sky stained in smoky gold and orange.

The silhouettes, Acel thought, would be something for an artist to sketch. Maybe some day I'll see a sketch like this and I'll have money then and will buy it.

Big Boy lay at Acel's side, his lips blubbering with his snoring. The newspaper he had held over his face had slipped onto his chest.

On Acel's left sat Bill, the newspaper reporter on the bum. Bill got up now and walked to the door. He was a short, trim man with a broad leather belt around his waist and a grey snapped-brim hat which had been trimmed with scissors. He leaned out over the silhouettes in the doorway, peered ahead, and then returned to Acel. "We'll be there in another half-hour, buddy," he said.

"Think it will be a good idea to get off before we get in the yards?" Acel said.

"This town isn't so hostile, but we'll get off anyway."

One of the silhouettes in the doorway pointed out to the Gulf, and pretty soon Acel saw it, too: the sails of a fishing boat, a tiny white thread on the horizon. He showed it to Bill, and the older man nodded.

"You needn't worry about eating in this town," Acel said. "I got a few nickels."

"That is all right. I got some change myself."

Acel shook Big Boy. "Hey, get up. We're gettin' in the yards. Get up."

Big Boy sat up and rubbed his mouth and chin and then began tying the laces on his shoes.

Acel looked through the doorway over the water again. A bum never lacks companionship, he thought. On every train there is a new buddy to pal up with, and in every jungle there's a bum going your way. A road buddy is someone to watch your bundle while you go get a drink or he dings the salt and bacon if you agree to get the pepper and bread. Maybe he has been over the route before, like Bill here, and knows whether the crews are tough or if there is a hard bull ahead. You can talk to a road buddy like you were talking to yourself. There were some good guys on the road. Take Bill here. Bill had had some good jobs and had been somebody. You could tell that by looking at him and the way he talked.

When the train entered the yards, Acel, Bill, and Big Boy jumped from the door and then waded through the tall grass of the right-of-way to the street.

"Let's don't walk right up through town," Big Boy said.

"I heard a cop say one time it was the bums walking around out in the residential districts that they suspected and picked up," Acel said. "I always just go through town like I owned it."

"You can't ever tell," Big Boy said.

"It doesn't make any difference to me," Bill said.

On the sidewalk ahead a group of children were playing, and the three men turned into the street in order not to interrupt their game. A little girl broke from the group and ran up the path to the house. "Some old bums, Mama. Some old bums," she cried.

Acel laughed. "You two shouldn't scare kids thataway."

"I think I'll holler boo at the little dickenses," Big Boy said.

"And have their old men out with shotguns," Bill said.

The jungle was a clearing in a woods of scrub oaks within a stone's throw of the railroad. It was strewn with blackened cans and empty rubbing-alcohol bottles. At its edge was a steep gully at the bottom of which ran a thin stream.

A dozen hoboes occupied the clearing. One of them had a mirror fixed in the bark of a tree and was shaving. A hobo, naked to the waist, came up out of the gully with a can of water. Big Boy lay on a spread of newspapers with his head wrapped in his coat. Acel and Bill sat on the edge of the gully looking down into the trickle of water.

"I'm getting fed up on this kind of life," Bill said.

Acel nodded. "It's pretty tough, all right."

"I'd rob a bank if I thought I could get away with it."

"You'll get a job, Bill. A man like you with those letters will get a job. I hate to see a guy like you on the bum. You're the first man, Bill, I've run across on the road in a long time that really thinks. They can call it what they want, Communism or Bolshevism or Socialism, but there is going to be a change. Men are not going to keep bumming or work in flop houses for ninety cents a week forever. Not when there are other men they can whip with their hands riding in Packards and giving twenty-dollar tips."

"I can sympathize with a man that steals. You must be a pretty good bum to keep in change like you do."

"Like I was telling you yesterday, Bill, if dividing the necessities of life up between men, food and shelter and clothing, is being red, then I am red as blood."

"The world galloped to Democracy and it may gallop to Communism some of these days. You can't ever tell. Everything dies. And that goes for countries and governments, too."

Two men in overalls and with cotton sacks on their shoulders came into the jungle. Acel lifted his hand in salute. The men sat down, and one of them opened a loaf of bread and split it into two parts.

"They don't know what it is all about, these bums," Acel said. "I talk to them, and all they can think about is where they're going to get their next lump or sack of tobacco. A revolution never will start among a bunch of bums. Sometimes I wonder if it's worth your time to talk to them about it all. Little matches make big fires, though. That's what a fellow I used to run around with would say. He's dead now. I thought a lot of that guy. But there's a million men in this country on the road, and if these men were organized or were prepared to follow some organization, it'd be something."

"I guess you have worked for some organization?"

"No, that's a funny thing, I never have. To tell the truth, Bill, I don't know what I am, except that I am a Socialist. That reminds me, I'll bet you could get a job on one of these Socialist papers. I wish I could write."

"I'm getting fed up on this, all right."

Acel pulled up his foot and examined the loosened sole of his shoe. "I'm going to have to get these fixed pretty soon. You got a good pair of shoes on you, Bill. These were white shoes I got on here, but I had them dyed."

"I may start north tonight to Birmingham," Bill said. "I know some fellows up there."

"I'd hate to see you go. Say, Bill, don't worry now. If you don't have anything in sight particular, just stick around with old Big Boy there and me. I'll tell you something on the quiet. Big Boy's got some dough. I've been with him more than a week now, and he sure is a good old boy. You stick around, and I'll see to it that you eat. He likes company, and we are going to New Orleans in a few days. I sure want to get over there, because I'm expecting some mail. I got a girl, see? I sent her a few dollars the other day."

"That partner of yours is a funny-looking bird," Bill said.

"Old Big Boy is okay. Funny thing, he's been in the bug house. Did you notice that scar? He's got a silver plate under it."

"I wonder how he got hold of that dough."

"I don't know."

"He's a funny-looking bird, all right."

Embers of the jungle fire blinked through the scrub oaks and brush. Sound of the hoboes' voices came to Acel as he cut across by the stock pens, the bundle under his arm, and made for the clearing. It was pitch dark.

There were more men in the jungle tonight than there had been that afternoon. There were three or four around the fire, but the rest lay scattered over the clearing, dark, unrecognizable, sleeping bundles.

"If one of you guys will get the water, I got coffee here," Acel said. The kid with the bandana handkerchief around his neck got up and picked up a can and disappeared in the gully.

"She'll come out on that third track," the hobo with the cotton sack around his shoulders said. "It'll be a 'leven-hundred engine. You wanta catch her back toward the crumby, though, 'cause there's always a bunch of empties up forward, and they'll set them off the first fifty miles down the road."

Acel took the can of water out of the Kid's hands and placed it on the fire. There was no use waking up Bill or Big Boy for coffee, he decided. They were sleeping some-where around.

"Have any of you guys ever had the syph?" Cotton Sack said.

"I've had the gon," the hobo with the black beard said.

"Soon as I get a few more dollars I'm going to Hot Springs," Cotton Sack said. "The government treats you there for nothing, I hear."

Acel placed more twigs around the can. Big Boy and Bill didn't drink much coffee, and there was no use waking them up. They had turned in awful early.

"I ran into a good place here about two months ago," Black Beard said. "I spots this house, and I says to myself, I'm going to ding this place if it's the last thing I do. It was a big white house, with flowers and things all over the yard. There was a big car out in front. I goes up to the front door, and a woman comes up. She was a good-lookin' woman and says, 'Come right in,' and I went in.

"She cooks me up a real feed, ham and eggs and two cups of coffee and some grape jelly. When I got through, she leads me to the bathroom and says for me to wash up and shave. There was a razor and everything in that bathroom, and I got all cleaned up and looking pretty good and come out, and she takes me to the bedroom, and there on the bed is a whole outfit, blue serge suit and shoes, and everything just fits me. I got all dressed up and went back in the parlor where she was, and she says to me, 'Did you see that car out in front?' and I said I did, and then she says I can drive it if I want to and stay there as long as I wanted to and have everything I wanted."

The Kid laughed. "Why didn't you stay?"

"I just didn't want to get tied down."

That guy is a big liar, Acel thought. He's just daydreamed that and is telling it for the truth now.

"I ran into a funny case here about two weeks ago on the highway out of Dallas," Cotton Sack said. "I was walking along, and a woman in a car stops and tells me to get in. We get to riding along, and she tells me she is going to El Paso to see her husband and got to talking about how she was hating to make the trip by herself. Just before we gets in Fort Worth she stops at a pig stand and gets a couple of sandwiches and some soda pop, and I gets another cigarette offa her. We gets into Fort Worth, and she says she has to see some friends there, and if I wanted to I could go out on the highway and when she come along she would pick me up. She gives me a quarter, and I gets a plate lunch. I was going to Big Spring, and I just went on down and got me a train, and I found out later that Big Spring was right on the way to El Paso and I could have rode with her easy enough. I never have figured out that woman, but you know how women are."

The water in the can began to simmer. "It won't be long now," Acel said.

The Kid got up and squatted beside Acel. "I got some coffee in my bundle if you need any."

"I got plenty," Acel said. "I got a whole lot in town."

"Which way you headed?" the Kid said.

"New Orleans, if I ever get there. I got a couple of part-ners sleeping over there, and I'm going to try and get them to go tomorrow."

"You can get it in New Orleans for a Poor Boy sandwich," Black Beard said. "That's how tough things are in that town."

"I had my first experience with a girl that had never been around this summer up in Idaho," the Kid said. "That's where I'm going now, back to Idaho."

"I guess you want to see her, all right," Acel said.

"I was working for her old man, and I kind of think he'll give me a job back. You know how they make fires at night up there in that country around the herd to keep the coy-otes away? . . . Well, she would set those fires at nights for her old man, and I'd meet her out there. I'd take a couple of blankets, and we'd stay out there doggone near all night. I kind of hated it on account of her brother. Him and me run around together."

"I got a girl, I know how it is," Acel said.

"Have any of you fellers heard about them going to stop train riding on the first?" Black Beard said.

"I've heard about it," Acel said. "What they're going to do is put up more transient houses, and you're supposed to stay in one spot. There's nothing but decent jobs that will stop men from running around."

"I don't like the way the birds in these Sallies and Munies order you around," Black Beard said. "They're nothing but bums themselves. I stayed in a few, but I'm not any more. Nothing but guys new on the road stay in those joints."

"They're no good," Acel said. "They can't get away with it long, working men six hours a day for ninety cents a week and rotten grub. The only thing that would make us worth a little more now would be a war. If some of the rich guys in this country decided we had to whip Japan or Germany or Russia, they would see to it that the government paid us a dollar a day and call us heroes to boot. Cannon fodder is worth a little more. But now we're worth ninety cents a week or nothing. If they ever want any of you guys to go and fight to save the world for Democracy, you tell them, 'No, thanks, it was saved once, and a couple of thousand men got richer and thirty or forty million got poorer.' I think this coffee is about ready."

"I wonder what the cops did with that guy they took away from here this afternoon," the Kid said.

"Were the cops down here?" Acel said.

"I knew that bird with that trick hat on was a dick," Black Beard said. "I've seen him on this road before. I knew he was a dick, and I had my eye on him the minute I got in this jungle."

"What bird is that?" Acel said.

"They're talking about that bird that had that dinky hat on, the one with that big belt on," the Kid said. "It was just before dark, just before you got here. Some cops come down here and took them off, but they say the guy with that hat on was a dick."

"Who did they take off?" Acel said.

"Some big old boy with a scar on his head. They put the bracelets on him. They searched us all, but they only took him. I thought we were all going to get run in, but they only took that big guy."

"The big guy, uh?" Acel said.

"That's the way they do now," Black Beard said. "I was up in New Mexico on a train one time and ridin' along with a guy, and he was telling me how he was a t.b. and everything, and damned if he didn't turn out to be a bull. He got a half-dozen guys on that train when they busted into a box car. I've seen that guy with that hat on before. I knew he was a dick. I had my eye on him the minute I hit this jungle."

23
WALKING PAPERS

THERE were four men in the small, L-shaped kitchen, three Negro workers and a white cook. The sweat on the dark skins of the Negroes stood out like blisters.

The cook had broad hips under the apron like a woman. "I don't know where we're going to put you," he said. "We got more back here now than we need."

"The manager told me to come back," Acel said.

"All right. Go over to Sam, there. Sam, give this man something to do."

"Ah'll give you an easy job," Sam said. "You can just do the glasses."

The white bus boys would bring the dirty dishes back and stack them on a table next to the swinging kitchen door. It was Acel's job to pick out the glasses and shake them in a pan of soapy, warm water. After that he stacked them on a tray and, when it was filled, carried it to the little window looking out over the dining room and tapped a bell for a bus boy.

Sometimes plates came back with half-eaten pieces of pie or cake, and Sam, the head dish washer, would hold it up and offer them to one of the other Negroes.

On the big iron range simmered a dozen pots. There was a long oilclothed table laden with pans of salads and cold meats.

Sam and the cook were talking. "It's not that Ah minds the foahteen hours in heah or the five bucks a week Ah gets, but Ah'm not gettin' the five bucks, and that's what Ah think Ah got a right to kick about."

"We're going to have a new deal in here," the cook said.

"We'ah gonna have somethin' or Ah'm not gonna stay," Sam said. "Ah work in heah all day and Ah gotta bum the tobacco Ah smoke."

The cook indicated the others in the kitchen with a twist of his head. "There's plenty in here that'll take your job. Any of these men in here would be glad to have your job."

"Whatsamatter? Ain't Ah doin' my work okay?"

"Sure, it's okay."

"All Ah was doin' was just kickin' about not gettin' paid. A man's got a right to kick about that."

The cook came over to Acel. "Well, how are you making it?"

"Okay. Say, chef, you know if they'll let you see a prisoner over in the county jail here?"

"You know 'em over there?"

"No, I don't. I don't guess they'd let me see anybody. No, I'm a stranger in town. Say, I wonder if I could work for my dinner tonight?"

"You oughten to be working for nothing. That's the trouble with things today, men working for nothing. This is a nigger's job, anyway."

Acel could see the clock in the dining room whenever the doors swung out, and now he saw that his two hours were up. There were two more glasses, and he washed these and arranged them on the tray. He folded the drying cloth carefully, hung it on the line, and then went over to the cook. "The manager said when I worked two hours I'd have a feed coming to me."

After he had eaten, Acel started for the courthouse across the street. It was a new, four-story building, with the windows of the fourth story barred.

There were two men in the sheriff's office. They had on wide-brimmed hats, and across their vests hung heavy gold chains. The one chewing the match came to the desk.

"I wonder if I could see a prisoner you got in here," Acel said.

"What's his name?"

"I don't know. You got him yesterday out at the edge of town. I'd like to know what you got him for."

"What is your name?" the officer asked.

"Stecker."

The officer spat out the match shred. "What are you doing hanging around this town for, anyway? I know about you."

"I been working across the street in that café. You can ask them. I worked over there for my breakfast."

"Now that you got your breakfast, the best thing for you to do is get on out of town. We don't want no Reds in this town. We got a pea farm for radicals like you. If you punks don't like this country, why don't you go back to New York, go back to Russia where you come from? Now you get out of here, and you keep going and don't you look back."

Mist played in the giant beam of the approaching locomotive. Acel, waiting on the steps of the sided caboose at the edge of the yards, shivered again. The engine puffed by, its fire boxes glowing, and Acel lowered himself to the ground. Then he moved across the tracks toward the mist- and night-blurred train.

The dripping runs were slippery, and Acel went up them cautiously, clasping each rung firmly and planting his feet securely. He climbed up onto the top and lay down on his stomach. The train jerked violently and then seemed to stretch in a sudden pick-up of speed. It began to rain.

This is pretty bad, Acel thought, riding in the rain like this, but you had to expect things like this when you were on the road. It was just six hours to New Orleans. Six hours, that was all. This is pretty tough, but it isn't like that train I held down up in Minnesota that February. That was a cattle car, and it rocked like a ship, and it was cold, and his eyes got filled with hot cinders. This wasn't anything to compare with that. That was really bad, because he had asked himself then if he had ever gone through anything worse: when they cut out his tonsils? When he got his hand mashed? This ride wasn't anything.

Water trickled from his hair and smarted in his eyes. The wet from the car's surface penetrated his clothes and placed a damp hand on his stomach. That's all I could do, Big Boy. It was me. I know it. I know it, Big Boy. I don't blame you. I know I am. You are right. I know I am. . . .

The whistle of the locomotive whined back through the rain.

24
NEW ORLEANS

ACEL came out of Jackson Square and stopped at the curb cart of colored bottles and ice. "Strawberry," he said, and the vendor shaved the ice, patted it into a paper cone, and sprinkled it with red flavoring. Acel handed him a penny.

On the pavement of darkened Chartres Street clung mirrory puddles from the evening shower. I'm going to walk clear to the end of this street. I like this street. I like New Orleans. It's kind of like a girl you have met two or three times and didn't think so much of and then all of a sudden you see her again and you want to hold her.

The shutters on this house sagged in all the windows. A dark passageway looked into a dimly lighted courtyard where four figures sat at a table playing cards.

I like this street. It's a street for a guy like me. It doesn't matter how you look or who you are on a street like this. It wipes its mouth on the back of its hand.

An old Negro sat in a chair on the sidewalk in front of his lamp-lit parlor and dozed. At the corner three men in work clothes came out of a place lettered: *Three Joes.*

I'm not feeling so bad tonight. That part of it all was for the best, and I didn't have any business thinking about it. It's just one of those things you couldn't do anything about, and that's all there is to it.

The girl sat alone on the stoop, her knees pressed together and the skirt held tighter under her legs. She did not look up. The sign read: *Tony's Second-hand Store.*

I have walked down a lot of streets, just moseying around like this. In Frisco and Minneapolis. In Denver and St. Louis. In little towns like Paducah and Ranger and St. Augustine. I have kind of liked them all and sort of hated to leave them. Each new town makes me forget the other. They're like girls.

A woman in the window of the building that looked like a school was placing shining linen on a bed. *Beer, 5¢. Poor Boy Sandwiches, 10¢.*

I feel better like this, in cotton pants and this old jacket and with two bits in my pocket, than I do when I'm dressed up and with a couple of dollars. When I'm dressed up I want tailor-mades and I see people with things and it makes me feel bad, but like this I don't care. I can flop right over there in that doorway if I want to, and two bits seems like a lot to me.

From the lighted, unoccupied room with its bed of twisted clothes came the smell of marihuana. The trolley rails glimmered up Royal Street to vanish into a blaze that was Canal. *Fishermen's Exchange.*

Old Hewitt would have given me a job if he had one. He was as nice as a man could be. A man can't give you a job unless he's got one to give, and he explained just how everything was and patted me on the back. If a man doesn't have a job to give, he certainly can't make one. *Hing Wo Long.* Just keep moving and you will always run into something. That was what that old bum in Omaha said. Just keep moving and something will turn up—a flop, a handout, a ride, a cigarette, a piece of change. All you had to do was keep moving.

The girl had blonde hair and a blue silk dress. The man looked like a Filipino. *The Golden Dragon.* It is kind of like Negro music, this night. It's like a trombone quivering something hot and sweet and then a muted trumpet harmonizing. . . .

The woman seated there on the shadowed steps looked up boldly and held his eyes. The rouge on her face was like brick dust.

"Hello," Acel said. "What are you doing here on this side street this time of night?"

"This isn't no side street. This is Royal."

"All these streets here on this side of New Orleans look like side streets to me," Acel said.

The woman moved a little to the side, and Acel lowered himself beside her on the steps. She had on a man's coat, and her black straw hat was pulled down over her ears.

"Must be getting pretty late," Acel said.

The woman nodded. "It's getting late, all right."

Feet scraped on the sidewalk, and they watched the approaching figure. It was a Negro, and he lurched past, head down and muttering.

"That jig is worried about something," Acel said.

"Some wench rolled him for his dough, I guess," the woman said.

"What are you waiting here for, trying to pick up some change?" Acel said.

"Maybe. Not particularly."

"I'm going to have to mosey on to the flop in a minute."

"Where you staying, kid?"

"Down the street yonder at Mom's Place. I was headed for it when I saw you."

"You got a place to stay, then."

"Uh huh. Why, don't you?"

The woman nodded. "Yes, I got a place. Right across the street there, that light up there. I've been staying with an old man."

"Old man, uh? How old is he?"

"Oh, he's past seventy. What I'm doing is sitting here trying to make up my mind whether to go up there or not. That bed of his is full of bugs."

"I don't guess a man that old bothers you, does he?"

"Naw, he doesn't bother me thataway. But he don't think

about anybody but himself. Spends all his money for drink-ing, and nobody else matters. Wine. He bought a gallon this morning."

Acel stroked the hairs on his forearm. "Uh," he sym-pathized.

"You're staying down at Mom's, you say? I know that old lady. She's a good old woman."

"Yeah, I moved in there this afternoon. It's pretty good for a buck and a half a week. This town sure is cheap. You can eat mighty cheap in this town, all right."

"I can't make up my mind whether to go up there to that old devil or not. That's what I've been sitting here for, trying to make up my mind."

"I wish I could help you."

"What kind of work you do for a living?"

"Christ, I'm not working. I'm on the bum. I looked up a fellow here this morning I used to play in a band with, and he put out a couple of bucks. I paid up my room and got a quarter left."

"Was he working?"

"The fellow I got the two bucks off of? . . . Sure. You know that circus that was here this afternoon? He was director of that band. I used to play in a dance band with him."

"Is that all you got off of him and him working? You oughta got more than that if he's working. You oughta got all you could have off of him."

"I guess I could have gotten more if I'd of asked him."

"They don't think about nobody, those people that's working and got money. That old man up there has some money, but he's the stingiest old devil that ever lived. *Wine*."

"It's pretty tough, all right." Acel ruffled the hairs on his forearm and began stroking them down again.

"So you're on the bum. Just go around from town to town, uh? How much money can you-all pick up a day?"

"Oh, I don't know. I'm not exactly a professional bum.

Some of them, though, pick up around two or three dollars a day, I guess. He has to work pretty hard, though, and don't let them ever kid you about a bum being lazy. That fellow I got that money off of this morning, though, I knew him. I've loaned him money."

"What do you do for women?"

"Just do without."

"Just go around from town to town, uh?"

"Sort of. I haven't been out on the road very long this trip. I left a girl I was living with up in New York."

"What is she doing now, living with her folks or something?"

"I don't know. She and I are washed up. I got a letter from her yesterday, but she and me are all washed up. It's for the best. Just one of those things, you know."

"I guess it is pretty good, just going around from town to town and seeing different things."

"It isn't so bad."

The lights in the window across the street went out.

"The old devil's getting in bed, I guess," the woman said. "You got a cigarette on you, kid?"

"I sure haven't. I just rolled my last one before I saw you. I got a quarter here, though, and I can go get us some tobacco. Where would there be a place open around here this time of night?"

"You'd have to go clear over by Market. No use of doing that. I wish I could make up my mind whether to go on up to that old devil or not. Wine he was drinking, and he wouldn't even give me the money to get something to eat."

"Haven't you had anything to eat?"

"I haven't had anything to eat today, and all he does is swill and swill."

"Hell, I got two bits here. Listen, you wait here and I'll go get some tobacco and this two bits changed."

"You won't come back?"

"Sure I will. Good god."

"You'll be back, then?"

"Sure."

In the café across the street from the Market, Acel bought a pack of Bugle. He got two dimes in change, and one of these he placed in his watch pocket and the other he carried in his hand. The stalks of bananas across the street at the Market corner gleamed. Acel went over and bought five for a nickel.

I shouldn't have bought these bananas. She'll think I'm a cheap skate bringing these back. If she hasn't eaten anything though, they'll taste good. When I'm hungry a banana looks good to me, by god. I'll give her this dime, anyway. I'll keep the tobacco and the nickel and in the morning get eggs at Young China.

She was not there. This was the place, all right; this was the stoop. But it could be that next block up there? . . .

No, that was the place back yonder. She was gone. That was all there was to it.

The window where the light had been was still dark. Acel put the dime in the pocket with the nickel and then opened the sack.

25
CLOSED DOOR

WHEN the Paul Whiteman program ended, Acel left the two young brothers, Lou and Wayne, at the radio in the parlor of Mom's Place and went out onto the gallery. Cook, the man who had a job coming up, was standing there looking across the street at the two girls on that balcony. The girls were fat, and every evening they sat on the gallery and rocked.

"Those gals are not going to give you any come-on," Acel said. "They know what kind of guys stay in this place."

Cook grunted. He was a man around thirty-five, with a body that bulged in the middle like a top.

Acel placed his elbows on the shaky balcony railing and looked down into the brick-paved street. A man in fuzzy white flannels and straw hat came around the corner, halted, and reached down and picked up a cigarette butt.

"I was around to the café again today, and he told me to come back," Cook said.

"He must mean business or he wouldn't be telling you to come back," Acel said.

"I got to hurry up and get something, because I can't wear these white pants in the winter."

"I look for you to get that job. He wouldn't be telling you to come back if he didn't mean business. I smell onions cooking somewhere, don't you? . . . That's one thing about you, Cook, is you've been looking for something to do in the line you know about. That's where I've messed myself up, fooling around with everything. That's what I've been telling the kids in there, a man ought to look for work in the thing he knows the best."

"This fellow has a pretty good joint. It's N.R.A."

"I hope you get on. Maybe you can work me in down there?"

"I'll do it if I can. I was reading in the paper over in the library this afternoon where the government is going to give a hundred thousand berries to this town to feed the bums on this winter. The government sure is going to help fellows. It's about time."

Acel shook the rail experimentally. "I saw that myself. Stabilizing transients, they call it. You're supposed to settle down in some place and quit riding around the country on freight trains. They're going to start vagging everybody they catch on the highways and around freight yards."

The mother of the two girls on the balcony came out with a platter of candy and handed it to each of them. A dog sniffed at the fire plug on the corner and trotted on.

"If they paid anything for cooking in one of those transient places, I wouldn't mind a job doing that," Cook said. "If they're allowing a dime a meal for each man, I can give them a lot better than I've seen. But hell, they expect you to work for nothing. You know how much those cooks over in Houston are getting? One dollar a week. And that's supposed to be the best place in the country."

Acel spat between his teeth over the railing and then looked to see if anybody was passing below. "It's tough, all right."

"I think I'm going to get a job, all right. He's got an N.R.A. sign up on his place, but of course you can't depend on that."

"Those girls over there never do look this way, do they?" Acel said.

"I could go for that one with the big bottom," Cook said. "Yeah, he was telling me today that the cooking was getting too much for his wife and he'd have to have a man pretty soon who was good on short orders."

Acel turned and faced Cook. "Well, I can't kick today. Mom sure did me a favor, putting me onto that nine bucks. I'd already borrowed four bits from her to get this suit out of the cleaner's. I sweated blood day before yesterday trying to raise a half-dollar to get this suit out. I went in one place right after another and offered to do anything. It's easier, by god, to bum four bits than it is to earn it."

"Nine dollars is a lot of money these days, all right."

"You don't need a buck, do you? I let the kids in there have a couple of bucks."

"No, I'm not busted yet. Did you know those kids in there before you got in New Orleans?"

"No, I just run into them like I did you. They used to play in some shows, and I know a few musicians they know. Dern nice kids."

Cook spat out a shred of fingernail. "Say, let's take a walk over in the Quarter and see what the gals are doing tonight."

"I don't care nothing about going over there. I don't have no business over there."

"C'mon. We don't have anything else to do, and it's too early to turn in. Looking isn't going to cost us anything."

"It don't appeal to me tonight. I don't like to go over there without I'm going to spend some money, and I'm not going to spend any of this."

"It won't hurt anything. Leave your dough with the kids and we'll just walk through and look at them."

They combed their heads, came out of the rooming house, and stood for several moments looking up at the girls across the street and then set out toward the Quarter.

"I was thinking that if some cop had come along last night I'd been in a hell of a fix while I was watching that house," Acel said. "I'd of had a swell time explaining what I was doing out there in the weeds of that vacant lot at twelve o'clock at night. Mom, I guess, though, could have got me out of a bad jam. That was an easy nine bucks, just watching a house to see who was going into it."

"That girl wanted to know if her sweetie was going in that house, uh?"

"Yeah. That's the first time I ever did do any detecting. I'd of looked good, though, if some cop had come along."

"How come Mom to put you onto that?"

"This girl knew her, see? I kind of hated to take the money from that girl. She works in a cleaning shop, and you know good and well she doesn't make hardly anything."

"That wouldn't worry me none."

They split and let the woman in the black dress and carrying a paper satchel go through.

"I could have had a job today," Acel said. "I'll bet you would have grabbed it up."

"What was that?"

"Posing. Dollar an hour."

"What kind of posing?"

"Naked posing. You know I thought about doing it there for a little while, but then I got to thinking. There was to be women there, too."

"You're not bulling, are you?"

"No, sir. That's a good racket here in the winter time when all the art schools are running. Mom was telling me she used to have three or four boys staying at her place who picked up four and five dollars a day posing. That was another thing about this job they called Mom up about. It was just for an hour. If it had been regular or something, I might have taken them up."

Three children stood around the penny-snowball cart waiting for the vendor to fill cones.

"If I'd been posin' and there was women there, it would

have been too bad," Cook said. "I could have made them a Nero. I'd pose naked before anybody for a dollar an hour."

"Mom was telling me they used to get fellows for the hospitals here. Doctors would use them for sterility tests. They gave them fifty cents for every test."

"If they furnished women it wouldn't be bad," Cook said.

They turned up a street of the Quarter. Women sat behind shuttered windows or stood in the cracks of partly opened doors and called and beckoned.

"Come here, darling."

"Sugah, come heah to me."

"I know you. I know you now. Come here!"

It was like flipping the leaves of a book, passing the crib-like brothels, escaping from the hawking voices.

A woman in a red silk dress reached out of her door and motioned. "Wait a minute, boys."

Cook shook his head and laughed. "Too late, sister. You're just a little too late."

They passed the old graveyard, leaving the Quarter behind; crossed the tracks and walked more slowly now toward their lodging place.

"That's not right," Acel said, "going down there without money and letting them yell at you. I feel like a Peeping Tom."

"What's the difference?"

"I heard a girl say one time that a down-and-out man became a bum and a woman turned whore."

"I don't feel sorry for them. They don't have no conscience, and they'll break up a man's home."

"I just don't know myself. I've quit thinking about it. I used to know a girl pretty well. I was kind of sweet on her, and that's what she's doing now. She didn't say so, but I could read between the lines, and I know good and well that is what she is doing. A man out of work doesn't have any business thinking about any kind of women. I lived with this girl awhile up in New York before she started it."

"Women are just born thataway," Cook said. "I don't have any use for them."

The white linens of the man approaching glistened. The girl with him clung to his arm with both hands and looked up into his face and smiled. Her face was soft and fresh and clean. Acel and Cook stepped into the street to give them passageway. Perfume lingered in their wake. Acel twisted his head and looked after them.

". . . The first thing on the menu always sells best," Cook went on. "If you have something you want to get rid of, just put it first on the menu and it'll sell every time. That guy must mean business, or he wouldn't be telling me to come back."

"I got a hunch you're going to get that job," Acel said. "I hope you do and get me a job. I wouldn't mind learning how to hash."

26
ACE'S FOUR VAGABONDS

LYING on the cot of his cell-like room, Acel stretched his arms and flattened his palms on the crumbling calcimine of the room's walls. It was that narrow, all right. Above the foot of the cot was a small, screened window looking on the scabby walls of an adjoining building. In the courtyard below the window, that kid next door was practising on his clarinet.

Acel looked at the soot-sprinkled bowl and pitcher on the washstand. The stand was covered with *Times-Picayunes*. I got the blues this morning. I'm feeling that way, and there is no reason for it, because nothing is different from what it was last night, and I was feeling pretty good then. My room rent is paid, and I got a few dollars, and there's no reason for it.

The clarinet squawked on the fourth note of the attempted scale.

No, I don't have a good reason for feeling blue this morning. The government is going to spend one hundred thousand dollars here this winter to set up free shelters and stabilize transients. That is a lot of money, and there ought to be some jobs. Thirty-dollar-a-month jobs. They are going to have to have some workers to register these bums and ask them questions. I could do that.

An ant crawled on the grey blanket, and Acel flicked it off with his middle finger and thumb.

It might not be a bad idea to look up that Mr. Jessup, the man, the papers said, who was head of the relief organization that was going to spend the money. That man will have to hire somebody. Not everybody is going to try and get jobs in a flop house, and I might get one. I believe I'll write him a letter. I could tell him that I'm pretty familiar with the way they run flop houses over this country and ought to be a help to him. *Dear Mr. Jessup: I see in the papers where you have been named director of the relief work for transients here this winter and it has occurred to me that I might be of some service to you in establishing these places. I am familiar with these shelters all over the country and know the various systems. I know the type of men you intend to help and I should be of some assistance in handling them. I have been having a pretty hard time and . . .*

No, it wouldn't do to tell him in the letter that I'm down and out, because they're not going to hire regular bums. They can get them for nothing, and they know it. He won't have to know anything except that I've been in college and look all right and am intelligent. I can look pretty good in that tweed, and he can talk to me and know that I can do that kind of work easy. . . .

I am a college man. Salary is no object. I realize you do not have much money to spend for salaries and for that reason I will be satisfied with a modest wage. . . .

Should I tell him thirty bucks? He'll think I'm pretty cheap if I say that, though. They may be planning on paying more than that, too. One thing is certain, he is going to have to hire men, because a man that has been secretary of a merchants' association isn't going to know much about bums, and he needs somebody that is familiar with them. I believe I'll say sixty dollars. No, I won't say anything. I'll just leave that up to him. . . .

I can take a conscientious interest in these men and assure you that I will work hard to make your welfare work here a success. . . .

That wouldn't be bad, a place to stay and thirty bucks a month. I'd feel like going around and getting acquainted with the musicians in this town then. If I stay in this town long enough, I'll run into a playing job. That's been my trouble, changing towns and not just keeping ding-donging at some of these bands. I could get me a horn if I got this job and get up a lip and sit in now and then with some of these bands and get acquainted, and the first thing I would have a job. I can't think about getting a horn, though, the first month. I ought to get an overcoat of some kind. I could get along without an overcoat down in this country, though.

The clarinet screeched on the sixth note.

I'd kind of like a job in a flop house registering transients. I could stay clean, and by spring I'd have some money saved. I wonder if there are many musicians on the road. There is Wayne and Lou. If four or five showed up around that shelter, we could organize us an orchestra. Say, that's an idea. If we had a sax and a piano, Wayne and Lou and I could have a band. That's an idea. I could call our-selves The Vagabonds. Ace's Four Vagabonds. That would be a good name. Maybe I should tell Jessup about that in this letter. That would make him sit up and take notice. Ace's Vagabonds. I can tell him all that, though, when I see him in person. But, by god, he ought to go for that.

It is my plan to call on you in a few days and I hope this letter will serve as an introduction. . . .

Acel got up and got the limp tailor-made out of the breast pocket of his shirt on the foot of the bed and after lighting it lay back down.

Now I'm getting ideas that will get a man somewhere. Ace's Four Vagabonds. I've been fooling around long enough and not thinking. I have to get women out of my mind and get down to business. An orchestra in a flop house that way could get publicity. We could get on the radio in no time at all. They would write us up in the papers: *Ace's Vagabonds, a novelty orchestra, made its début over Station KLRN here last night. The band featured melodies and songs of hobo camps and trails. One of the songs, "Thg Flop House Blues," was written by its director, Acel E. Stecker. The orchestra is to be booked for stage appearances . . .*

Now I'm having good ideas. Wayne can play baritone, and Lou plays bass and doubles on the banjo. Lou's got a pretty good voice, too, and he and I can do some duets. I'll look up some hobo songs with good harmony. . . .

I will await your reply hopefully and now I beg to remain, very respectfully, Acel E. Stecker.

Acel got up and, putting on trousers and undershirt and shoes, went out onto the gallery to get the socks he had hung out. Mom, the woman who ran the rooming house, and the Baroness were in the courtyard below. The two old women were poking in a heap of cans and flower pots. Mom saw Acel and beckoned.

"Wait till I put on a shirt," Acel said.

Mom smiled as Acel approached. "Now you said you wanted to meet a real live baroness, here's your chance, young man. Baroness, this is one of my boys. He's a musical young man."

"How do you do?" the baroness said. The powder on the stiff black silk bosom looked like flour, and it lay, too, a scaly crust, on her wrinkled throat underneath the high lace collar. "I love geraniums," the Baroness said. She exhibited the flower. "I just love these. Do you know where I could get some more, my boy?"

"I could look around for you, Baroness," Acel said.

Mom indicated the pile of cans and pots. "We were looking for a pot to plant this geranium in."

"Maybe I can find you one." Acel bent down and began picking up and examining pots.

Mom was a smaller and more shriveled woman than the Baroness, though she was younger. She moved in sparrowlike hops. It was said that she had once been a wealthy woman and a society belle. She had never married. She and the Baroness had known each other in their youth, and now the Baroness, it was said, was dependent on Mom.

"If you want to do something for the Baroness," Mom said, "you can go get some dirt. I think that pot there will do. I saw some earth down on the corner where they are fixing up that sewer. Take that pot and fill it up, and then you can take it up to the Baroness' room. She would like for you to visit her awhile, wouldn't you, Baroness?"

"I just love geraniums," the Baroness said. "In France I had millions of them. Oh, millions." She looked at Acel and shook her head sadly. "But no more, my boy, no more."

The Baroness occupied the choice, front bedroom of Mom's Place. It was a linoleum-floored room with a white iron bed covered with a rose-colored cotton counterpane. There was a washstand with a marble top, and a huge brown wardrobe, and a brown dresser on which stood an oil lamp.

The Baroness was seated in a rocker with a cloth-bound scrapbook in her hands when Acel entered with the filled pot. "Now where do you want me to put this, Baroness?"

"Are you a gardener, my boy?"

"I'm afraid I'm not."

"Just put it out on the gallery, then. Mom will fix it for me."

The Baroness showed Acel the scrapbook. It contained a number of big, slick photographs, and these the old woman handed to Acel one at a time.

"I was in the moving pictures once, you know," she said.

She was in these pictures, all right. Here she was a lady-in-waiting to the star queen, and here in a ballroom and here at a banquet table. She looked like royalty, all right. She looked as regal as the actors and actresses.

"Here I am, see? I was acting in this picture, just a little part, you know, but I was really employed as a technical adviser. Oh, it was such hard work. I was at the studio all day, and at nights I was so exhausted. I had been in Hawaii, and when I arrived in Los Angeles they called me up and asked me to be what they call a technical adviser. Oh, it was such hard work. Fifty dollars a week they paid me. I did not like it at all, it was such hard work."

"You look about twenty years old here." Acel tapped the picture.

"That is what everyone says. Now everyone says I look so much younger than Mom, but do you know that I am seven years older than she? Now don't you tell her I said that, because it makes her very angry when anyone says that."

"You sure look young, all right."

"I hope you understand me. Some people do not understand me so well, though until three years ago, until I moved here from California, I taught expression. I taught a bunch of young men once in Hawaii. I lived in Europe so long, you know, but I was born right here in this country. I was such a little thing when I went to Europe. Oh, it was so long ago. It was a wonderful little town and the most beautiful château that my husband took me to. The Baron, you know. But I have nothing now, my boy, nothing."

Acel eased a little down in the chair.

The old woman brought out a sheet of paper from the scrapbook. "Would you like to see this that is written about me? . . . It was written by the dearest little girl who took expression from me. She was a typist, you know, worked in an office, I think it was, and she wrote this about my life. My wedding, rather. She was a dear little thing. I understand that some magazine would pay a lot of money for this. I told her about the wedding, and she wrote it up, and I would like for some magazine to pay me for it."

Acel took the sheet of paper. It was typewritten and single-spaced: "Not so many years ago in Europe occurred a wedding of great importance. It joined two distinguished families, one on this continent and one of the Old World. Just a little slip of a girl left her American home and journeyed across the deep sea to be united in holy bonds of matrimony with a member of one of Europe's most distinguished royal families. The little girl . . ."

Acel read it all and then handed it back to her. "This is very interesting, Baroness. Very interesting."

"Oh, it was a wonderful wedding. The horns went ta-ra-ta-ta." The Baroness cupped her hands to her mouth. "The horns went ta-ra-ta-ta, like that. And there were so many flowers. Oh, they were so beautiful. My husband was so handsome. That is his picture there on the wall. Oh, it was wonderful. The horns went ta-ra-ta-ta."

Acel got up and went over and looked at the photograph in the round frame on the wall. It was of a young man in military uniform, standing stiffly with his hand resting on the back of a carved chair.

"In Paris we had our own box at the opera. Thousands we had then, oh, thousands. I could have my friends, and, oh, I could give away so much." She shook her head and fixed her eyes on Acel. "But I have nothing now, my boy, nothing."

Acel sat down again.

"Do you know of a magazine that would buy this article? The little girl said that there would be many magazines that would pay money for it. Oh, it was a wonderful wedding. Do you know of a magazine?"

"Not one that I can think of right off."

"Oh, it was marvelous. The horns went ta-ra-ta-ta, like that."

Acel cleared his throat. "How come you to lose your money?"

"The war, my boy. We had everything, our own box in the opera, and I gave away thousands to my servants. We had wine. Oh, so much wine. But I have nothing now, my boy, nothing."

"I guess it must be pretty hard to have had a lot of money and then lose it all."

"What is that? Sometimes I do not hear so well. Oh, it was a wonderful wedding."

"I say it must be pretty hard to lose everything."

"Oh, you have no idea. And the people in this world are becoming so cruel. When I was a little girl, the people were kind to one another and helped each other, but the world has changed. These politicians are the cause of it all. These Republicans and Democrats. My boy, don't ever have anything to do with men like them."

"I guess monarchies are about as good as anything," Acel said. "I used to be interested in things like that, but what I'm interested in right now is an orchestra I'm planning on organizing."

"Oh, you have no idea. I have a little money, but it is nothing. I get fifteen dollars a month from some property I have in Florida, but do not tell anyone that now. Every month when I get my money I buy avocados. I love avocados. I bought two lots in California for fifteen hundred dollars apiece, and you know they told me that they would be worth five thousand dollars, but I have only been offered one thousand for the both of them."

"Yes, you sure look young in that picture there, Baroness."

"It was taken eight years ago. That is what everyone says. Do you know about these advertisements endorsing face powders? You know, I would do that now. I am not proud any more, my boy. I need money. Do you know how to go about that? I would not mind."

"I'm afraid I don't, Baroness."

"I need money, my boy."

"It must be pretty hard, all right, to have had a lot and then lose it all."

"Oh, we had so much. He's been dead so long now. We had so much wine. Mom likes whisky, but I do not care for whisky. In Europe my husband had cellars of wine. Oh, we had so much. The cellars were just filled with wines and brandies and champagne. But I have nothing now, my boy, nothing. Not even a little wine."

Acel shifted in his chair. "I guess I ought to be going, Baroness." He got up.

"I love gin, though. Do you know where I could get a little gin, my boy?"

27
LOU AND WAYNE

Lou was twenty-four and the older of the two brothers. He walked loosely, his chin down, and shot quick glances at passers-by. Wayne, twenty, was larger in build, a smooth-muscled giant with the clear complexion of a child. The eyes of women lingered on Wayne.

The brothers dressed alike, corduroy trousers and faded, neckless jersey sweaters which clung tightly and outlined their big chest muscles. They were musicians and for two years trouped with carnival bands, but the last show got six weeks behind with their pay and they quit. In New Orleans they had been soliciting shoe-repair work for an Italian shoemaker for twenty-five per cent commission.

"I hate the houses where the niggers come to the door and say the lady of the house isn't in," Lou said. "I feel like telling them to go to hell, I want the lady of the house, not them."

"That was a nigger that gave us all those shoes Monday," Wayne said. "Four dollars' worth, that was. I guess you remember that."

"One place out of about a million. What I think we ought to do is get out of this town and go to California. That is the place for all of us. I promise you two that I'll hit every bakery between here and L. A."

Acel shook his head. "No, I keep telling you two that I

got a deal on here that's liable to bring us all three something. I want to let that letter soak in a little, and then I'll go up and see him. You two stick around now, and if I get in with these people I can fix you up. We can pick up a sax and a piano, maybe, and have a pretty good outfit. There are possibilities to this idea of mine."

Lou stared across the park toward the Pointalba Building moodily. "There's nothing in this town. You don't have a horn, Ace, even if that guy gave you a job, and ours are in Chicago."

"I'm not worrying about a horn. If I get in with these people I can get a horn soon enough, all right."

The sun blazed blindingly beyond the statue of General Jackson and above the Cabildo. A man in his shirt sleeves on the next bench peeled a peach. A woman in an overwashed, bile-green dress and wrinkled hose went by.

Lou got up. "I guess you two could eat, all right, if I went and got something off a bakery."

Wayne grinned. "Sure, go get us something to eat."

Lou looked at Acel. "That's the way with him. He won't bum nothing himself, but it's okay for me to do it."

"He's your kid brother," Acel said. "You got to look out after him."

"I notice both of you always eat what I bum, but I don't see you-all bumming around."

"You're the best bum," Acel said. "We admit it, don't we, Wayne?"

"Get me some cream puffs," Wayne said.

"I'll take jelly doughnuts," Acel said.

"You goddamned guys give me a pain," Lou said. He turned and stalked around the park path and disappeared on Chartres Street.

"That bud of yours is a funny guy," Acel said.

Wayne nodded. "Uh huh."

"I was afraid he was going to get us in a jam this morning with that copper. You can't afford to jaw with cops like that when you're on the bum. It's a wonder he didn't run us in."

"He hates cops to beat hell. Ever since that time up in Kentucky he sure don't like them."

"What happened up in Kentucky?"

"Some cops gave him a dirty deal up there. Constables, I mean. It was the time he came down to see me when I was visiting an uncle of ours on his farm. He'd been playing in a little old dance band back home and had him about sixty bucks saved up, and he came down to see me."

A young couple went by looking straight ahead. The fellow had a box camera.

"How did he run into constables?" Acel said.

"They were looking for a gangster to show up in that town from Indianapolis, and Lou looked like him and he was from Indianapolis, and so they put him in the calaboose. They took his money off of him and used most of it up telephoning long-distance and sending telegrams. They found out the next morning he wasn't the one and let him loose, but they had spent his money, most of it, and scared him to boot, and it sure made him sore. You ought to hear him tell about it."

"I'll be damned."

"And I'd already gone home, because I didn't know he was coming, and old Lou had to catch a freight train out of there to get home."

"Can you beat that!"

Lou came around the walk carrying a loaf of French bread like a club. He pitched it suddenly, and Wayne caught it. "I guess they think a man can live on bread," Lou said. "I hit four places, and that's all I got, the damned cheap skates."

"Did you ask them to let you work?" Acel said.

"Not me. I been hooked too much that way. You remember that guy in Charlotte, don't you, Wayne?"

Wayne nodded. "Tell old Ace about that."

"We run into a smart guy up in Charlotte last spring when we quit that show. I saw him gettin' out of a new Ford, and I went over and hit him up. He tells me he'll give me two bits if I change his spare. I started in taking the spare off, see? And then I says, 'Which one of these wheels do you want me to put this on?' and he says, 'Any of them.' I says, 'Don't none of these need changing?' and he says, 'Naw, I just believe a man oughta earn the money he gets even if he has to just pile rocks from one pile to another.' I let that spare drop then and I told him to go to hell."

"What did he do then?" Acel said.

"He turned white as a sheet and then just went on in the restaurant."

Acel laughed. "It's a wonder he didn't call a cop."

"He didn't have the guts to do anything, did he, Wayne?"

Wayne broke the twisted loaf in three hunks. "Uh huh."

"That's a good-looking suit you got on there, Ace," Wayne said. "I wish I had a good front like that."

"I got this when I was working on that boat up in New York. A man should keep a good front, all right. I'll need this tomorrow when I see that fellow Jessup. I didn't shave this morning, because that razor blade of mine is just about good for one more decent shave, and I want to look like something when I see him tomorrow."

"I wish I had seaman's papers like you," Wayne said. "I've always wanted to go to South America."

"A college boy with a letter to a shipping master has a better chance of getting out than an A.B.," Acel said. "When things pick up, though, a ship ought to be pretty easy to get. When times are good they can't get seamen in this country. That's what they tell me. They got to get a bunch of foreigners to run American ships."

Wayne scraped off some dried mud on the cuffs of his trousers with his fingernail. "I've always wanted to go to South America."

Acel stood up and shoved his hands deep into his pockets. "You can't ever tell. Something good might come out of me seeing this Jessup. They're going to need some help, all right."

"With a good front like you got on you, you might get something," Wayne said. "I'm going to get me a suit if I have to start paying it out fifty cents a week. We ought to be out now trying to get some shoe work, Lou."

"This town isn't no good," Lou said. "Listen, you guys, we can ride the T.P. outa here to Fort Worth and then catch it out there clear to El Paso. That's a run for you, from Fort Worth to El Paso. It makes passenger time."

"I've made that trip," Acel said.

"Or we could ride the I.C. outa here up to Memphis and cut across Arkansas if we're not in a hurry," Lou said. "That's a state I never been in. I been all around, but I never have made Arkansas, and I wouldn't mind doing it just to say I had."

"What do you keep talking about leaving for?" Acel said. "This town isn't so bad. It's the cheapest town in the country."

"Show me what's good about it!"

"You know yourself now, Lou, that when you got out in California you'd stick there a couple of months and then you'd wanta start for some place else. Just about New Orleans, too. That's the trouble with us fellows, we're always wanting to go on and not sticking in one place long enough to run into something. I've decided I'm going to get back into the music racket if I have to get religion and join a Salvation Army band. You ought to be pumping a bass again, Lou, and making some licks on that banjo. There's nothing to this runnin' around, I'm tellin' you."

"No, I don't think we ought to go to Cal," Wayne said. "If we went anywhere we ought to go back up to Chicago. Sis said she'd stake us to some money if we came up there. I'd like to get a new suit. I'm tired of wearing these damned corduroys."

"Well, I'm not going home," Lou said. "There's nothing in that little old town, and the old man has all he can feed without the rest of us sticking our feet under the table, too."

"I don't want to go home, either, but there's nothing for us in Cal, and we could get a few dollars in Chicago from Sis."

"You two just stick around here for a while," Acel said. "There's nothing to this moving just to be moving."

Lou tried to spit across the walk. "I hear the bulls are gettin' pretty hostile around Memphis."

28
HOBO SPECIAL

THE ice cream soda, Acel thought, would be a good investment. He had not spent anything for breakfast, and he needed something on his stomach before he went up to see Mr. Jessup. There was nutrition in chocolate ice cream, and five cents was cheap enough. But he was not hungry. That was it. But the soda would make him feel more fresh, and he needed to feel fresh when he approached Mr. Jessup.

It made him feel brighter, all right. But he had chumped off, paying that blonde cashier, and bought tailor-mades. If he had quit at the soda and bought Bull Durham it would have been all right, but he had chumped off and spent twenty cents. I can't hold onto money, that's all there is to it. And I don't even have that soap yet. Well, I can just keep on using laundry soap. A man who'll chump off like I do doesn't deserve anything else but laundry soap to shave with.

The offices of the Transient Relief Director in the tall building had a bare, just-moved-in look. There was a woman typing at a desk just inside the door, and she told Acel the man at the desk in the corner was Mr. Jessup, but that he was busy now and Acel could sit down and wait.

Acel sat on the bench against the wall near the door. Mr. Jessup was talking to a young man, a fellow with a Roman nose and horn-rimmed glasses. The young fellow's head went up and down as Mr. Jessup talked. Mr. Jessup was a middle-aged man with a grey face. The lapels of his coat were decorated with civic club buttons.

"I am taking it for granted, of course, that you are coming with us?" Mr. Jessup said.

"Oh, sure, sure, sure." The head of the young man went up and down. "Yessiree."

"You think you can line things up all right?"

"Oh, sure, sure, sure. Yessiree."

There was another worker in the office besides the woman, a man with white hair and of Mr. Jessup's age. He had been dusting a typewriter, and now he put the cloth down and studied the table on which the machine rested speculatively.

"Can I help you, Frank?" Mr. Jessup called.

"I think I'll move this table a bit," White Hair said.

Mr. Jessup got up and so did the young man and the woman typist, and they went over and all of them moved the table.

Returning to his desk, Mr. Jessup paused before Acel. "Did you want to see me?"

"Yessir." Acel stood up. "I wrote you a letter. I am Acel Stecker, I suppose you read it, all right?"

"I am glad to know you. I am very, very busy this morning. What was it, now, you wanted? I don't believe I recall the letter."

"I wrote you a letter. It was about a job."

"Oh, I see. Then you want to see that man right over there. The gentleman there. He handles our employment. Go right over there, he's your man."

White Hair paused in the ribbon running with Acel's approach. "It's a little hard to tell you about it, because I tried to explain to Mr. Jessup in a letter, and of course you know nothing about the letter. I'd like to have a job in one of these transient houses you are going to put up here. I'm pretty familiar with that work, and I thought you might be going to put on housemen."

White Hair yanked out the top drawer of his desk and from a broad pad tore off a blue form on which was printed at the top: *The State of Louisiana.*

"Fill that out," White Hair said. He returned to the ribbon running.

Acel studied the question form. There were a lot of questions, and one of them asked how long the applicant had been a resident of Louisiana.

Acel returned to White Hair. "Does this mean you have to have a poll-tax receipt before you can work in a flop house?"

"Not only that, but you must have two poll-tax receipts and also be a legal resident of this parish as well."

"That lets me out," Acel said. He placed the blue form on White Hair's desk and turned and walked out.

The sun was hot on Canal Street, and Acel took off his coat and loosened his tie and collar. There's no use of cussing about it. There's no use of doing anything. Forget it . . . forget it . . . forget it. . . .

The two brothers, Lou and Wayne, sat up on the park grass eagerly.

Acel spread his hands emptily. "Nothing."

"Did you see him?" Wayne said.

"Yeah, I saw him. It's all over, finished." He brought out the pack of cigarettes. "Have one, you two."

"Where did you get those tailor-mades?" Lou said.

"I chumped off. Go ahead and take one."

"What did that guy say?" Wayne said.

"You got to have a poll tax and be a voter and things like that. I'm always making a mess of things. All the time. I'll swear, that's all I can do, is make a complete mess of everything I do."

"The sons of bitches," Lou said. "They got a hundred thousand bucks, and all the bums will get is some mush with weevils in it and a damned cot full of bugs."

"All I'm good for is to make a mess out of things. You

guys oughten to be running around with me. I'm telling you, I'll make a mess out of things for you. I make a mess out of things for myself and for anybody that has anything to do with me."

"What I'd like to do is join these Communists," Lou said. "When are these Communists going to do something, Ace? How do you get in with that bunch, anyway?"

"It won't do you no good," Acel said.

"I wish somebody would start something," Lou said.

"We were talking to a fellow just before you got here," Wayne said. "He just got out of the can. They vagged him last night in Lafayette Square, and he was going to leave this afternoon on the S.P. He sure did have it in for this town, didn't he, Lou?"

The heels of a passing girl in a white spring coat clicked on the walk. "I wouldn't mind taking that girl out yonder," Acel said.

"The engineer stops for the bums on that S.P. train outa Gretna every morning," Lou said. "They call it the Hobo Special. They say they stop to let everybody on."

"We're not riding any trains west out of here," Wayne said. "That I.C. hot shot that goes out of here about five o'clock in the morning is a Hobo Special, too."

Lou pinched off his cigarette and put the snipe in his pocket. "We could make it to Chicago in three days. Memphis is the only big town we got to get through."

"I wouldn't mind going to Chicago myself," Wayne said.

"How in the hell are we going to pass away the time in this damned town between now and in the morning?" Acel said.

29
CHICAGO

BETWEEN the shores of Michigan Avenue spectators the military band came like a golden-crested wave. The silver slides of trombones glistened in tearing smears. French horns, the melody-drowning drums, clarinets, trumpets passed.

Lou nudged Acel. "That's something I wouldn't play. Cymbals. If I had to rap them things I wouldn't play in a band."

Acel smiled. The band passed, and in a few moments its melody ended in shrill of trumpets. The feet of the following marchers, carrying N.R.A. signs, scraped harshly on the pavement. "I'm about ready to check out," Acel said. "How about you-all?"

They squeezed through the bank of spectators and emerged in a clear area on the sidewalk in front of a men's furnishing store.

"I hope this N.R.A. gets over," Acel said. "Maybe we'll all have jobs pretty soon."

Wayne went over and looked in the show window and then beckoned.

"C'mere, you guys. This isn't bad, is it? Fourteen ninety-five is all, too."

They looked at the suit. It was a blue suit with white pin stripes.

"If I didn't look so much like a tramp, I'd go around to where Sis works and get that money there," Wayne said. "I hate to go up to the house tonight, because that old man of hers might be there."

"If I ever get a job I'm going to see to it that she quits that guy," Lou said. "He don't want her helping her own brothers. She's working and making her own money, and I don't see that he's got any kick coming."

"He'll be at the union meeting tonight," Wayne said. "I told Sis not to even let him know we were in town. You're going out there with us tonight, Ace. Sis is a swell girl. She won't care how you look or who you are."

"I'll just let you two go."

They walked on up the street and after a while turned into Grant Park. The parkscape stretched in a green, street-grooved shaft to end in the shining masonry of the Field Museum.

They dropped on the grass and began rolling cigarettes. "I been thinking about that army band," Acel said. "I wouldn't mind being in a band like that. They don't have such a bad time."

"It'll be a cold day in hell when I join the army," Lou said.

"We was in the National Guard one summer," Wayne said. "That's why we joined the carnival, to keep from going the next summer. If you're out of the state, see? you don't have to go."

"I see you in the army, Ace," Lou said. "You'd get a bellyful of it pretty quick taking orders around. I'll bet a man couldn't get in it, though. There was a couple of fellows in the show with us that tried it, and they told them that the army was full up with musicians."

"Aw, I was just thinking about it," Acel said.

The sky over the lake was like frozen bluing water. Wayne pointed, and pretty soon they saw the airplane, too, and nodded.

"If I had a horn and you guys got yours, we could fire

us up a little German band," Acel said. "Bass, baritone, and trumpet. You could get some strings for that banjo, Lou, and we could work us up a few songs. I saw some of those bands in New York in the spring, and they looked to me like they were picking up quite a few nickels. Liquor is bringing them back."

"I wonder how much they pick up a day," Wayne said.

"More than we're picking up," Lou said.

"I watched them last spring around over on the East Side in New York. They play little German tunes and 'Good Old Summertime' and 'Sidewalks of New York' and tunes like that. I'll betcha we could start picking up a few dollars a day like that."

"They just pass the hat around, uh?" Wayne said.

"Listen, you guys," Lou said. "I'm not going to be the only one passing the hat, see?"

"What I want to do is start making some money before it gets cold," Acel said. "It's going to be winter here the first thing you know, and we're going to be S.O.L."

"We can go to California," Lou said.

"I wonder how much you could get a horn for," Wayne said.

"I don't know," Acel said. "You can get them for nothing now, almost."

"I'll bet you wouldn't play in a band like that," Wayne said.

"Shoot, I'd start out in the morning with you guys."

"I'm going to keep five bucks out of this money Sis gives us for a suit," Wayne said, "but I don't care what you guys do with the rest. Why don't you get you a horn, Ace, and we'll start this thing up?"

A tall, long-waisted man in striped work trousers and a soiled white shirt that billowed over his belt approached them.

"Here comes old One Eye," Wayne said.

One Eye had on new tan shoes. "Which one of you guys got a smoke on you?" he said.

Wayne handed him up the tobacco sack. One Eye rolled the cigarette and then seated himself. He had a grey glass eye. "How about a match, one of you?" he said.

Wayne turned and spat between his teeth with an upward jerk of his head. Acel handed One Eye a match.

One Eye pulled out a bottle from his bosom and began scraping off its transparent covering with his fingernail. It was labeled: *Rubbing Alcohol.* He unscrewed the blue cap and extended the bottle, but the three younger men shook their heads. One Eye tilted the bottle to his mouth, and the fluid rushed in foamy beads through the bottle's neck.

"I don't see how you drink that stuff," Wayne said.

"It's better than jake." One Eye screwed the cap back on and put the bottle back in his bosom.

"What was you doing to that old man over in that car on the avenue?" Acel said. "Puttin' the bing on him?"

"Yeah. Did you see me? I scared the hell out of that old man. I told him, by god, I hadn't eaten in two days and I had to have some money to eat on. He forked over a half-buck."

"You got the bowels, all right," Acel said.

"That's what it takes to get by on in this world, pal. If you don't ask for it, you don't get it. I'll bum the hell out of 'em."

"I'd rather work for mine," Acel said.

"I got a pal that's got the right idea," One Eye said. "He ain't nobody's fool, that guy ain't. He says the guys that stay in these flop houses and work all day for ninety cents a week are scabs. Dirty scabs. Bum it, that's what I say. Bum 'em until the people know something is wrong with this damned country. That's the way they can fix this country up until it amounts to something."

"You sound like an I.W.W.," Acel said.

"What do you know about the I.W.W.?" One Eye said.

"One of those I Want Work guys."

"That's what you know about it, uh? That's what guys like you know about it."

"I probably know a helluva lot more about it than you do."

"Ho, you're a smart guy." One Eye brought out the bottle and took another drink. The lids around the glass eye were fiery. "Lot you know about it. Where's your card?"

"You think you have to have a card to know about it?"

"Ho, you're a smart guy. Know all about it. When the revolution comes, smart guys like you are liable to know a helluva lot more about it." One Eye made a slitting gesture with his forefinger across his throat. "Like that."

"Old Booger Red himself," Acel said.

One Eye got up. "Smart guys." He stood there for a moment and then turned and walked away. His shirt tail was out.

"I'll bet he's as strong as an ox," Wayne said.

"If I couldn't whip a derail like him I'd kiss anything you say," Lou said. "These Reds are a bunch of dopes."

"He's all smoked up," Acel said. "He's too radical."

30
". . . GOOD OLD SUMMERTIME"

ACEL STECKER leaned against the lamppost, pitching the mouthpiece of the cornet up and down on the palm of his hand. Lou and Wayne were under the Elevated waiting for the traffic to clear to join him.

"If we pick up two more bucks today I'll ask Suzanne to go to a movie with me tonight, Acel thought. She'll go, all right. I can tell that she will go with me, all right. I got to take her to a show or something though the first night. A man has to have money when he starts out with a girl. It'll be all right to be broke some later on, but going with a girl the first time or two you got to have a little money.

Suzanne has been around. Girls in cafés have been around, but Suzanne isn't but nineteen, and she hasn't been around much. You could tell that in her eyes. Corinne's eyes got hard at times, but she was older, and she had been around a whole lot. She had been around too much, and you could tell it in a girl's eyes. I'll say to Suzanne tonight: "Would you like to go with me to a movie tonight when you get off, Suzanne?"

Wayne stepped up onto the sidewalk. "We going to make a stand here, Ace?"

"No, not here. I thought we'd take a turn around that

corner yonder and play the backs of some of those apartments. This is a good time of day."

Lou dragged up. He pushed the banjo back on his shoulder and lifted the bass horn and, pressing the spit valve, blew into the mouthpiece. The saliva in the instrument made a gurgling sound.

"A drunken guy jerked loose with four bits over there," Lou said. "I like to dropped dead."

"We're doing pretty good today," Acel said.

A man smoking a pipe stopped and looked at them and smiled. The clerk in the delicatessen peered through the window.

They moved on up the street, Wayne and Acel walking abreast and Lou behind.

The taxi driver waiting for the green light leaned out of his cab window: "Hey, how about a tune, boys?"

Acel and Wayne smiled and saluted and shook their heads. "Go on and peddle your moonshine," Lou shouted.

"I wish we were working toward Madison instead of thisaway," Wayne said. "I'd like to put this two bucks I got in on that suit while I got it."

"Listen, Ace," Lou said. "Let's make Jim's Place again tonight. That's a good bunch around there. I wouldn't mind gettin' drunk again tonight myself."

"And puke all night like you did the last time," Wayne said.

The girl in the short fur jacket and mesh hose smiled as she passed. Wayne turned and looked after her.

"There you go," Acel said, "gettin' your mind off your business. You got female trouble, that's what's the matter with you."

"She wasn't looking at me, she was looking at you," Wayne said.

"Women don't look at me no more since I been running around with you two punks. You're the sheik, Wayne."

"You're the one that's got female trouble. How about

Suzanne? When you going to take that girl out, anyway? You're the one that's got female trouble."

They turned into the rear courtyard of the apartment building, into a canyon six stories high. Two children came up out of the basement steps and watched. A poodle on a leash jumped up and started barking. A woman with a towel around her head and a cloth in her hand stood at an opened window on the second floor and looked. Acel lifted his cap to her, and the woman smiled.

A window on the left raised, and a man in a smoking jacket leaned out, with his hands on the sill. He turned and then held a child up to the window.

Acel lifted his cornet. " 'Good Old,' " he said, "and put the pecks in, Wayne."

After that they played "There'll Be A Hot Time," and now there were a dozen figures in the windows.

Lou set his bass horn down and loosened his banjo. He and Acel sang "Down by the Old Mill Stream." Coins wrapped in brown sack paper and newspaper dropped into the courtyards from the windows, and Wayne went around and picked them up.

" 'Sweet Adeline,' " the man in the smoking jacket called down.

They sang that, and then Lou picked up his bass and pushed his banjo back and they moved out of the courtyard.

"That bastard in that jacket just gave us a dime," Wayne said.

"Did that woman with that towel around her head pitch anything down?" Acel said.

"A quarter."

"I figured she would."

One Eye was standing in front of the cigar store on the corner. There was a man with him, a short man with a Hitler mustache and checkered trousers and blue coat.

"I thought that was you," One Eye said. His good eye

was as glassy as the other with drink. "Ho, strike us up a
tune."

" 'The International,' " Hitler Mustache said.

"That's it," One Eye said. " 'International.' We'll give you
a nickel."

"Go to hell," Acel said.

One Eye lurched out and grasped Acel's arm. Acel jerked
away, and the cornet fell from under his arm and clattered
with a tinny sound on the sidewalk.

"You goddam fool," Acel said. He struck at One Eye's
face with his fists, struck at it again . . . again. . . .

A circle was growing around them. One Eye clutched
Acel and clung, and Acel struggled to extricate himself and
strike with his fists. One Eye dragged him down and lay
on top of Acel. People crowded closer, their feet in the
faces of the fighters. One Eye lay on Acel's chest, his chin
digging into Acel's flesh. Acel hit at his ear. . . .

The circle widened suddenly, and then the policeman
was yanking at One Eye's collar. One Eye clung tighter,
and then the officer struck One Eye on the back with his
stick. . . .

The policeman stood between One Eye and Acel on the
curb, waiting for the wagon. One Eye's nose was bleeding.
He held one hand over his glass eye.

"Where are you going to take this fellow?" Lou asked
the officer. "We want to testify for him. That one-eyed guy
there started it every bit. We were just walking along, and
he started it every bit."

"You got my horn all right, haven't you, Lou?" Acel
said.

"I got it. Officer, I'm telling you that we were just walking
along here, and that guy started it."

The police wagon smelled of disinfectant, like a jail. Acel
sat forward on the bench, and One Eye back. They did not
look at one another.

This blood I got on me is off of him. I'm not bleeding

nowhere. I don't remember him hittin' me a time. Aw, Christ, I would get into something like this. I have the hardest luck of any man in this country. I never did see anything like it. I'll swear . . .

One Eye gagged and then began to vomit on the floor.

31
"THE INTERNATIONAL"

THE judge on the high bench was a fat, youngish man with long black hair brushed back across his temples and with a shaved, red neck. Sometimes he would lean forward, his broad, cleft chin resting in his left hand, and when he straightened he ran his hand through his hair.

From time to time the clerk read names, and one of the shabby men on the long bench with Acel and One Eye would get up and stand before the judge, and then in a few minutes they would cross the room and sit on a bench on the other side.

If I could just have shaved this morning I wouldn't look so much like a tramp, Acel thought. I'm going to shake when I stand up there. I'm going to have court fright. If I could have just shaved, then I wouldn't mind it. *I'm not guilty, your honor. If you will permit me, your honor, I will tell you just how it happened, and then if the court believes I am guilty I will take my punishment.*

I'll get it in the neck, though. Thirty days, and I might just as well get ready for it. I expect to get it, all right, and if I do get out of it with less than that I'll have something to feel good about. Thirty days? It'll be cold when I come out and me without an overcoat, and I'll have this six bucks I got spent by the time I get out. Lou and Wayne will head for California as sure as hell. Well, I can go to California as soon as I get out. I'll hang onto this six bucks and have something to start out on.

The judge will know I am no ordinary bum when I address him. He will know that by the language I use. *Your honor, my companions are here in the courtroom now, and they will testify that we were just walking along there, minding our own business, and this man steps out and starts trouble.* The judge will know by the language I use that I am no ordinary bum in court for fighting on the street. . . .

The clerk called "Acel Stecker."

One Eye followed Acel to stand before the bar. He had a handkerchief tied across his bad eye. The policeman was there, too, his cheeks round and puffed like shined apples.

One Eye said he was guilty, and then the clerk motioned with his thumb and One Eye went over and sat on the bench on the other side.

Acel's eyes shimmied in their sockets. He looked at the judge and struggled to keep his eyes steady. "I'm not guilty, your honor."

The policeman spoke with jerks of his head. "They tied up traffic around that corner for fifteen or twenty minutes, and it took me quite a while to clear it up. They were both fighting. This fellow here is a street musician, and they got into a fight over what they were going to play."

The judge jerked a hair out of his nose and then looked down at Acel.

"I'll tell you, Judge, just how it happened. The fellows that play with me are here in the court, too, and they can tell you just what I tell you. We got a little, and we been trying to make a living by playing around on the streets, and we were coming by this corner and that man over there steps out with another fellow and asks us to play 'The International,' and we——"

"The what?"

"The Communist song."

"I see. Go on."

"I told him we wouldn't do it, and we were going on, and then he jumped out and jerked my horn out of my hands, and it fell on the sidewalk, and the first thing I was protecting myself. We don't make very much, and I can't afford to buy new horns, and so we started fighting. I didn't want to fight, but he grabbed me and I couldn't do anything else but protect myself."

"How old are you?"

"Twenty-six."

"What kind of a band is this you have?"

"It's what you call a little German band, but one of the boys plays banjo and we do some singing. We're just trying to make a living."

"Why wouldn't you play 'The International'?"

"That tune? We don't play tunes like that."

The judge straightened in his swivel chair, looked around over the courtroom, and then leaned forward again. "I do not excuse street fighting. It is dangerous to the safety of innocent passers-by and a public nuisance and menace. However, there is something significant in this case, and I wonder if you realize its significance, too. But I am sure that you do. The fact that you refused to play the hymn or the song, or whatever it is, of a corrupt foreign country is significant and a patriotic gesture to me that deserves consideration."

Acel struggled to control the shimmying of his eyes. The judge raised his voice:

"Communism is an organized effort to overthrow the democratic governments of this world. 'The Star-Spangled Banner' stands for liberty and justice and freedom, but that song stands for the interbreeding of Negroes and whites and Mongolians and Hindus, and it stirs up riots and bloodshed and sabotage and civil war. It means the destruction of courts meting out justice and trials by jury and would set up a dictatorship of the unintelligent classes and crush the skilled worker and the professional man and the man who appreciates the finer things of life. I am going to let you go this time."

"Thank you, judge."

The clerk read another name.

Lou and Wayne were waiting in the corridor outside the courtroom. "Boy, you sure made a speech," Wayne said. "Boy, you sure did tell it to him. Boy, that was good."

"You-all didn't say anything to Suzanne about me getting in jail, did you?"

"No, sir," Wayne said.

"Let's get the hell out of this place," Acel said.

The man in the double-breasted suit with the handkerchief in his breast pocket who had leaned against the bar beside the judge halted them. "How long you boys had this band?" he said.

"About two months now, I guess," Acel said.

"You just play American tunes? Is that the idea?"

Acel nodded. "What are you, a reporter?"

"Yes. I'm planning on doing a little feature about you boys. I'd like to get your pictures, with your horns and things. Can you get to your horns right away?"

"Aw, don't put nothing in the paper about this," Acel said.

"Why not? I've got a photographer coming, and we'll shoot you around here some place. What I want to do, though, is put you boys onto something. I'm in charge of a program for a veterans' smoker Friday night, and I want you boys on it. I'll see to it that your pickings are good. You ought to pick up fifty bucks or so in a bunch like that. You fellows wait here now until I go back in here and get a few names."

They looked at the closed doors of the courtroom through which the reporter had gone. "I don't guess that guy is horsin' us, is he, Ace?" Lou said.

"He was a reporter, all right. Say, we'll look hot in a picture, won't we? That's pretty good."

"I'd like to see that fifty bucks he was talking about," Wayne said. "I wonder if he was bulling."

"He's not bullin'," Acel said. "Listen, you guys, we got a name from now on, see? The Three Americans. We got to get up some war songs, Lou. 'Over There' and 'Tipperary' and stuff like that, see? Break your necks when this reporter comes back. He'll get us in the papers, and that's publicity. If we play at this smoker, I know damn well we can get some more jobs. That reminds me, we got to get up a dirty song or two. A mademoiselle song or two. I got some ideas, by god."